EXECUTIVE
BONE YARD

A Novel of Betrayal,
Greed and Shattered Dreams

EXECUTIVE BONE YARD

A Novel of Betrayal, Greed and Shattered Dreams

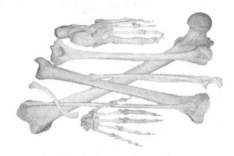

Michael A. Sisti

OH!
ORSINI
HOUSE

Executive Bone Yard
A Novel of Betrayal,
Greed and Shattered Dreams

Cover Design by Michael A. Sisti
Cover Illustration by Bogdan Bungarden
Text Design by Michael A. Sisti
and Sara O. Sisti

Reviews are the lifeblood of every author. After you have read this book, I would sincerely appreciate it if you would write a brief review on the site you purchased it, or on Goodreads.com. And if you have friends and family that would enjoy this book, please tell them about it.

*This book is dedicated
to all the entrepreneurs
who built their businesses
with their financial and sweat
equity and lost them, either
through the economic impact of
the Covid pandemic, or at the
hands of unscrupulous
predators.*

Prologue – The Heist
October, 1993, San Bernardino, CA

At 7:45 pm, Harold Payne was alone, agitated and pacing. He was aimlessly wandering throughout the nondescript warehouse production offices that were furnished with twenty-year-old battered metal desks and decorated with days-old coffee cups, cluttered files and overflowing ashtrays. Pride and caring left these premises a long time ago.

Impatient by nature, Payne's anger was boiling over as he waited for the trucks due nearly two hours ago. Venting and cursing, he threw one of the half-filled coffee cups at the grimy schedule board on the back wall.

Every minute was critical. If they didn't arrive soon, the massive cargo consignment would never get loaded in time. He was sweating profusely at the thought this delay might ripple through his entire plan and cause him to miss his meticulously planned getaway.

But then, hearing the hiss of the air brakes, he rushed to the loading dock and raised the two overhead doors. The first driver casually walked back from his cab and climbed onto the platform. In a spray of spittle, Payne shouted his frustration, screaming at him. "What the fuck happened to you? You should've been here two hours ago."

"What can I tell ya? Traffic was bad. You shoulda seen it. The rain musta caused six different accidents. I'm talkin' serious pileups."

The casual response only angered him further. "Don't fucking bullshit me. If you thought there were a couple of whores waiting for you, you would have been here early. So, where's the fucking pelican cases?"

"I got 'em in the cab. I'll bring them right out."

The driver of the second truck strolled up to the platform. "You ready for us to begin with the loading?" His easy-going drawl only poured gasoline on the fire.

Payne was now approaching heart-attack territory. "I was fucking ready two hours ago. I even rented a second forklift so you could load two trucks at a time." He then told the drivers to take every pallet in the warehouse which he had estimated to be four trailer loads.

Seeing the two pelican cases dropped on the platform calmed Payne down. While the truckers loaded the pallets, he toted the two heavy-duty plastic packing boxes into the office.

Grinning, he unlocked them, checked the contents and counted the bundles of large denomination bills. When he finished at $3 million, he sat back and relaxed. His plan was working just as he had envisioned it. Besides these two cases of cash, he had already skimmed another $2 million from the company. This would set him up for life.

Harold Payne was a forty-year-old former attorney, who had given up his mediocre law practice to salvage his deceased client's business. His well-worn black tailored suit and frayed, monogrammed dress shirt harkened back to a time when he was a hugely successful Los Angeles power lawyer, and weighed at least a dozen pounds less than his ample 190 pounds.

Despite his height at five foot, five, he was an imposing man with greying temples contrasting his black hair and full beard. Ebony-rimmed glasses framed his dark glowering eyes, sunken under a black bushy eyebrow stretching clear across his forehead. The intensity of his impenetrable stare caused discomfort in anyone he addressed.

The only time Payne ever smiled was when he was telling one of his tasteless, chauvinistic jokes. His idea of humor was feminine-degrading, off-color sexual metaphors. This was in sharp conflict with his fastidious grooming. However, his custom-tailored apparel had seen better days when his income was hundreds of thousands of dollars higher.

Less than an hour later, The Brazilian showed up. He was of medium height and wiry, with athletic moves both efficient and intimidating. His swarthy color, facial expression and body language exuded a harsh sense of impending terror, making anyone in his presence nervous and uncomfortable. Almost no one knew his real name, which was Diego Santos. His underworld contacts referred to him simply as *The Brazilian*.

When he strode into the office, he nodded to Payne, saw the two cases, and walked over to test their weight. He smiled and said with his slight accent, "Okay, if it's all here, then let's go."

Payne replied, "The money is all there, but we can't leave yet. They haven't finished loading."

"Fuck them. We've got the money, so who cares if they finish or not." He picked up the cases and hustled out the front door. Payne grabbed his briefcase and a small carry-on bag and followed him out of the building.

They climbed in The Brazilian's rental car and drove to a small airport where they boarded a chartered Lear jet with a flight plan to San Juan, Puerto Rico. Once they were in flight, Diego handed Payne a packet of documents with a new identity and a new cell phone. The passport photo showed Payne without the beard and glasses.

With a sinister smile, Diego addressed Payne, "Adios, Harold Payne. We mourn your passing. It is a pleasure to meet you, Gerard Morbus.

"Remember Gerard, you must never answer to Harold Payne again. It's important to work on that. Get used to being called Gerard Morbus. Your life will depend on it."

The Brazilian then explained the next steps of the journey. "We will land at a private terminal at the airport. Leave everything on board, except your carry-on."

"What about the money?"

"A car will take you to the main terminal and bring you back to the plane. When you get there, go directly to the men's room, shave off the beard, change your clothes, and

3

put on this hat. Come back out the same terminal door. The car will wait to take you back to the plane," he ordered.

"What about my glasses?"

"Toss the glasses and put in your contacts. Once you're back on board, I will leave, and the plane will take you to your destination. Upon arrival, my sister, Salete Pereira will be there to meet you and bring you to your new apartment.

"She has the name of the bank where she deposited your other funds under your new name. You are to give her the pelican cases, and she will process the cash into your new account." He spoke crisply without interruption.

"Salete will also help you get acclimated to your new surroundings. When I next visit that wonderful city of my birth, we will meet for a drink."

"Diego, assuming everything goes as planned, when you come to visit, I will have a $50,000 bonus for you," offered Gerard.

"That is most kind of you, sir."

"I am not being kind. I am truly impressed with the professional way you have managed this entire operation. And I'm looking forward to my new life in an exotic part of the world."

And while the prospects sounded exciting, would Gerard be up for the unknown challenges ahead?

1

The Trade Show
March 2016, Las Vegas, NV

Riding a taxi up the Strip in Vegas for the first time, Dave Powers was bombarded by the architecture, and the chrome and neon glitter designed to overwhelm the senses. He didn't need this artificial stimulation to drive his exhilaration. He was pumped.

Powers was in Las Vegas because he had negotiated the largest contract in his company's history. The firm he co-founded, HydroDyne Technologies, marketed a patented system that significantly reduced water usage in hotels and multi-family apartment buildings. They sold the system through distributors in the plumbing field.

His new client was the fastest-growing plumbing franchise firm in the country. What made the deal so sweet was that his system was being very heavily promoted by the franchise operator, who had a financial stake in its sales.

The kickoff of their trade show was tonight, with expected attendance of over 500 franchise plumbing contractors. The VP who signed his distribution agreement had arranged for Powers to have a corner booth on the center aisle of the exhibit hall. And he also featured the HydroDyne System in the show directory.

Over the next few days, Powers planned to demonstrate his system to these prospects. If a mere 5% of them purchased the system, it would far exceed the best sales month in the seven-year history of his firm. And he needed to make a big score at this show. The survival of his company hung in the balance. This critical fact hung over him, but through the enthusiasm of the VP, he was confident this event would be like Black Friday at Kmart.

Dave Powers was in his mid-seventies, an age when most men were well into their retirement. When asked about stepping down, he often told his wife, "I'll retire when it stops being fun." His active lifestyle, with a healthy mix of skiing, tennis and golf, kept him in excellent physical shape and looking a lot younger than his years. Powers wore a constant smile and was always ready to share one of his quirky observations of the activities surrounding him. It was the character trait that defined his sense of humor.

As the cab pulled up to the front entrance of Caesar's Palace, Powers jumped out, grabbed his carry-on and rushed into the lobby. The check-in area, next to the casino, was jammed with people from every corner of the world. They were all caught up in the artificial frenzy created by an atmosphere filled with flashing lights, ringing bells. The hopeful, chattering people and the mesmerizing energy added to Powers' excitement and expectation he was about to hit the jackpot.

After checking in, Powers went to the trade show ballroom. He was shocked to find it in total disarray. It wasn't close to being ready for the opening in less than four hours. He found his booth location with his display still in crates, and his display material missing.

He sought the floor director and shared his plight, which was the same as everyone else's. The director radioed the storage room and in 20 minutes, he had his cartons and a union team to set up his booth.

At 6 pm, the doors opened, and it was showtime. The plumbers swarmed in, hungry for deals and anything free, as they walked the aisles to discover new products. This was their first opportunity to see HydroDyne's system, and they all flocked to Powers' booth.

Over the next three hours and all the following day and a half, he did countless demonstrations, which impressed every attendee. They played with the device, asked questions, and congratulated Powers on his marvelous system.

By the end of the show, not one plumber out of 500 who saw the demo made a purchase. The letdown for Powers was devastating. He could not understand, despite all the hype, he didn't even get one sale. Upon his return, he would have to confront the franchise company's VP to find out why.

He didn't sleep on the red-eye flight back to Florida. He kept going over in his mind each sales pitch and every demo, trying to determine how he failed to make a sale. It crushed his confidence. Without some major development, his company was on the verge of collapsing.

2

Facing Reality
March 2016, Sarasota, FL

On Monday morning at 7:30, Powers arrived at his office after the disastrous trade show ending Friday. His upbeat personality and usual keen intent to start the day's work were severely hampered today.

He had spent the weekend alone with his wife, Elisa, brooding over his failure at the show, discussing with her the consequences ahead for them. By all expectations their newly upgraded product should have been the trade show's big hit. Instead, it bombed.

His company was now in danger of closing. And this would be catastrophic. Facing the strong possibility of this grim future, Powers kept trying to console his wife. However, he had no encouraging scenarios to offer.

Powers met Elisa at a ski and cycle club nearly 40 years ago. Despite her shyness, she was immediately caught up in his fun-loving demeanor and risk-taking sense of adventure. She was a freelance graphic designer who had never married. Blessed by her Italian heritage, Elisa had sparkling hazel-green eyes, contrasted by dark brown hair and the most beautiful olive complexion. Her five-foot frame was nicely proportioned with gentle curves. She proved to be a smart business thinker and quickly became her husband's sounding board and advisor.

"David, what will we do if the company fails? We have no money."

"I have a backup plan. I'll get a job as a Greeter at Walmart."

Laughing, she answered, "I should have expected that. You just can't have a conversation without injecting your humor. But seriously, what are we going to do?"

"I'm going to make HydroDyne successful. I don't know how, but I will get it done."

Powers was in the final stages of a lengthy career. He had founded nearly 20 companies and was a recognized industry expert with national acclaim in the marketing field. Having lost a substantial portion of their retirement portfolio during the economic collapse in 2008, they were both reluctant to get involved in the formation of HydroDyne the following year.

The business relationship had started as a new creative assignment, one they desperately needed for their marketing consulting business. Unfortunately, the startup team had no money and offered Powers stock in the soon-to-be-formed company for his critical services. After learning about the water-saving performance of the invention, he agreed to design the graphics, and write the marketing plan.

Learning the features of the product, Powers recognized its huge potential in a world facing climate change. As a serial entrepreneur, he could not pass up this opportunity, despite his age and shaky financial position. He was a risk-taker and had confidence he could always overcome any adversity.

And now, after seven years, he and his partner Ronald Lawson had yet to draw a salary as they continued to further invest in the company. This had been the worst possible time for Powers to partner with Lawson and launch this new venture.

The firm's potential demise troubled him. He felt he had no choice but to succeed. Failure was not an option. He had no time to rebuild his retirement portfolio. HydroDyne was all he had left. But it was out of money with no prospects to pay back his investment.

Powers was uncharacteristically immobilized with fear. He and his wife had already sold their home in a gated country club community and were now renting an apartment. They sold their cars and leased them, to raise more cash. Even with those drastic steps, they would run out of money in the next few years. There was no way he could let Elisa down after she had put her trust in him in every venture they launched over the past 35 years. He would find a way out of this mess.

3

Board Meeting Tension

Well, there was no fun in today's forecast. In a couple of hours, Powers was scheduled to update the company's other two board members on the recent sales performance.

He had to share his disappointment in the total failure at the previous week's trade show. And he would have to report on all his sales efforts, explaining why the recently upgraded product was not selling. They all had expected it to catapult the company at the forefront of plumbing technology. And to their dismay, orders were not emerging.

As sales and marketing VP, the responsibility for the success of the system's distribution was ultimately his. However, the lack of funds for even a minimal marketing effort stymied his efforts. But funding alone would not turn the revolutionary system into a winner. They had all miscalculated their target market.

Since its founding, the company couldn't convince the plumbing contractors to recommend and install this breakthrough water-saving system. The plumbers concluded it would substantially reduce their inbound service calls. Despite that fear, the industry experts all claimed the system was so good, it would eventually catch on.

Right from the beginning, all the sales, as anemic as they were, came solely from Powers' email and cold calls. They were barely enough to keep the company afloat. And through all this time, he couldn't solve the marketing challenge that would change the plumbers' attitudes about his system.

11

The three board members met as if they were mourners at a funeral. Besides the two founders, the trio included Paul Hedges, a retired executive from a major water heater manufacturer. They met in the conference room of the firm's small headquarters office. Despite the quality used furniture throughout the space, the absence of wall décor and other amenities, plus the hollow birch doors and well-worn, cheap carpet were a telling sign of the company's financial plight.

Ronald Lawson had worked closely with the inventor of the company's original product, a complex technology system that reduced water consumption in large residential properties and hotels. It could cut water volumes by 30% or more.

Lawson had provided most of the half-million-dollar startup money through his family's trust. Powers brought Hedges to the team as a consultant to provide his insights into the plumbing industry from his lengthy career.

At the time of the launch, most of the early participants including the inventor declined to become investors and join the new venture. Lawson and Powers moved ahead on their own and formed the company with small investments from a few of the others.

They invited Hedges to invest and become a board member. Both partners thought his lengthy career in the plumbing field and his industry knowledge would help propel the company into the market. They also felt he could attract other investors to become shareholders.

What they hadn't known was that Hedges' father had used his contacts to land his underachieving son the plush position at the water heater company. And, like so many other bureaucrats, Hedges spent his entire forty-five years at the firm without a single significant accomplishment.

Paul Hedges was a six-feet-tall, gaunt individual with a stooped-over posture. He had thinning gray hair, small bulging eyes and a hawk nose. His skin looked like it had never seen the sun. And he wore a constant expression that gave the impression he had spent the last hour sucking on a lemon.

Hedges was considering an investment but was reluctant to commit. The partners agreed to add him to the board, confident he would become a shareholder. Yet, despite awarding him a block of stock equivalent to the expected investment, he never put up any money. And this had become a flashpoint with Lawson and Powers.

Lawson opened the board meeting at 10 am, looking very nervous. He was 62, with a slight frame and a tanned body. He was good looking with brown hair and blue eyes. Lawson, divorced for over 20 years, had a friendly smile and was an easy conversationalist. Considered a trust-fund baby, his uninspired career included oversight of his family's trusts through a major regional bank; dabbling in a few small business ventures that were all unsuccessful; and his role as the caretaker for his aging father, the patriarch of his family.

His role with the company included administration, procurement, and logistics, none of which he excelled in. The firm's sales were so small that even a neophyte like him could complete the mundane tasks. He still mangled the books and the inventory.

Lawson began with the discouraging financial report. After spending tens of thousands of dollars developing and producing the new, more advanced product, sales did not materialize. Without new orders, the company was rapidly going broke. He explained that unless there was an immediate turnaround, they must take drastic steps to keep the company afloat.

Powers was aware of the dire situation as he and Lawson discussed it daily. Conditions were so grim they were considering the extreme strategy of moving the inventory to a storage facility, closing the office, and working from their homes.

Powers was second on the agenda, reporting on the dismal sales. He also shared the bleak details of the expensive trade show in Vegas, which did not produce a single order.

Hedges, who had not kept up with the company's progress, was shocked and enraged. His lengthy career had been with just the one company, a dominant player in the field. Its popular product line, with its volume-pricing position, enjoyed world-wide distribution within the plumbing supply channel. Also, as a bureaucrat, he really didn't understand the entrepreneur model, and how it functioned. This background rendered him all but useless as a member of the HydroDyne board.

Unable to contribute anything meaningful, Hedges blustered at Powers, "Where are the orders? Why aren't the plumbers buying our system? Sales are your responsibility. This is your damn problem, so what are you doing about getting business?"

Not expecting this kind of reaction from Hedges, Powers uncharacteristically came back strong with his response. "Paul, if we're going to point fingers, let's start with your $100,000 investment the company never received. I could have used that money to promote some quick sales and establish proof of concept."

"Why would I invest my money in this firm run by two amateurs? You still haven't gotten through to the plumbing contractors."

"Last week, I was face-to-face with 500 plumbers, for chrissakes. They won't buy our system. Why? You're the industry expert here. You can't come up with a reason why. And you want to lay this problem on me? Why are you even here?"

Lawson, soft-spoken and never adversarial, piled on with his own reaction.

"Paul, Dave is right. We gave you 50,000 shares of stock for your investment and your knowledge, and you've delivered nothing. You offer no advice, but you always criticize us. We need cash now, so step up and pay for your stock."

"Under these circumstances, I wouldn't put a cent into this company. You've squandered all the other investment money, and we're practically bankrupt. Did you spend it all on yourselves?"

Powers exploded. "That's total bullshit, Paul! How dare you even think it?" he shot back. "Ronald and I have not taken a paycheck in the seven years we've been in business. Instead, we write checks to the company to keep it going. My wife, Elisa is owed $25,000 for all the graphic design and production work she's done over the years. The company can't even reimburse us for our expenses."

"I never agreed to invest. I accepted stock for my value to the company, my expertise, and my resumé. The two of you should have had no trouble raising additional capital with my name on the board."

Powers interrupted, "Do you believe your resumé is worth 50,000 shares? It hasn't attracted one potential investor. And your so-called expertise has never helped our sales strategy. You are a sad, self-absorbed dreamer!"

Hedges ignored the dig. "Dave, you're supposed to be a sales and marketing expert, and yet you can't take an innovative product and sell it. Did you ever consider that the plumbers may fear the unintended consequences of installing a product like this? And Ronald, I've been worried about you from the beginning. You're not CEO material and you have no track record of success. I expected your failure from the very beginning. I never understood why you didn't quit when you realized you were in over your head."

Stammering from this unexpected put-down, Lawson jumped up and gathered his paperwork. Addressing Hedges, he said, "This, this meeting is over. I work my butt off. Without compensation, I might add. And the only mistake I made was accepting you on the board. Now I've got some real work to do."

As he turned to leave, his thick file folder dropped to the floor. He quickly picked up the dozens of color photographs of game fish and high-end motor yachts. Without missing a beat, stormed back to his office.

At the same, Hedges rose, shook his head and prepared to leave. Before he could, Powers turned to him. "Paul, we're sick and tired of your criticism whenever you happen to show up for a meeting. Ronald is right. If you continue to refuse to put up your investment, then return the stock and resign from the board. And do it now!"

Hedges walked out of the building without a word, leaving Powers frustrated.

4

A Dropped Clue

When Lawson left for lunch, Powers sat alone in the office, fuming over the immature behavior of his two associates. Faced with the impending shuttering of the firm, all they could do is bicker. That left him to salvage the company with some immediate sales, and without any help from either of them. He must be more productive making cold calls with no promotional support.

Powers recognized that his strength was his marketing skills, and while he had been both a sales executive and sales manager in the past, he was not a pure, gifted salesperson, someone who could sell ice to penguins on a glacier.

With the finality of the looming peril hanging over them, he had expected a better outcome from his associates. They faced bankruptcy. And neither of them could come up with one suggestion to salvage their situation. This left him very agitated. The issue that had prayed on his mind all weekend was still plaguing him.

Both Lawson and Hedges were financially set for life. It would not be a catastrophic event for them if the firm failed. But for him and Elisa, the company's demise would be a life-changing event. He couldn't imagine his future without some long-term income from the company, or at least, recover his investment.

Powers had invested much less cash in the company than Lawson, but his contribution to the firm's survival was immeasurable. Lawson held substantially more stock than Powers, which reflected his larger investment. However, his frequent errors in bookkeeping, purchasing and logistics cost the company significantly, partially offsetting his monetary investment.

When he finally pulled out of his funk, Powers realized that he had to rescue the company himself. Negative thinking wouldn't cut it. And neither would his two associates. He had to find the solution.

Then, remembering Paul Hedges' comment, he jumped up and shouted to no one, "That's the answer! It's been staring us in the face all this time."

It was galling that it had taken Hedges over seven years to contribute his first idea to help the firm. And he wasn't even aware that he had done it. It further confirmed that his stock was unearned. Powers decided he would reaffirm his demand to return the shares.

Hedges' throwaway comment was the key to unlocking their marketing strategy. The plumbing contractors were afraid that if they install the system, their future repair business would dry up. He had to convince them that the system would bring them new customers. Their business would grow, not shrink.

This message would get the contractors' attention and drive sales. Now, where was he going to get the money to communicate it to the plumbers? And did he have the time to make enough sales to stabilize the company?

5

Stress Relief

Following the meeting's abrupt ending, Lawson walked back to his office, incensed. Hedges' insulting treatment of him struck a nerve. The phone rang. It was his girlfriend calling him. "Hi Ronald, so how did the meeting go? You were so anxious when you left my place this morning. I wanted to check up on you."

"Sally, it was a disaster. Paul Hedges came in and was very abusive. He just doesn't understand the importance of my role."

"But you're the CEO. That's the most important job in the company. You manage the operation. Doesn't he get that?"

"He's not only clueless how I literally run everything but the sales, he doesn't recognize that I put up most of the money to finance this company. And he refuses to pay for the shares we gave him. I can't tell you how angry I am over this."

"Oh, Sweetie, try and relax. He's not worth the stress. I'll get a good bottle of wine and make you dinner tonight. See you about 6."

The call calmed him down. And he thought what a wonderful partner she made. At least, she recognized the importance of his contribution to the firm. She also knew about his $500,000 initial investment, and the subsequent cash infusions of $25,000 that were so critical.

Her call reinforced his opinion that he was doing a good job with the admin and other responsibilities. He admitted to himself that he was rather uncomfortable with the accounting, but he had to control the books. It wasn't a matter of trust, as he had unflinching confidence in Powers' honesty. It was more about the lessons his father taught him so many years ago. His advice back then was, "*When you control the money, you hold the power.*"

In reflection, Lawson convinced himself Hedges was unfair in his criticism. However, he never once considered his lack of contribution to the strategic planning and to the constant challenges facing a CEO.

That afternoon a call came in from Costa Rica. It thrust him back to the previous year. Lawson had met Carlos Diaz, the owner of a tourist resort during a fishing trip down to a small village on the Pacific Ocean. In their initial conversation, he mentioned his company and their newest product that was being introduced. Lawson then had Powers follow up with product literature and a sales pitch to install the equipment on the hotel property.

Following the call, Lawson ran into Powers' office to announce the good news. The vacation property in Costa Rica was ready to go ahead with their installation. This would be the first customer to buy their new system.

Lawson had already been planning another vacation to this fishing resort, but their gloomy financial situation held him back from mentioning it. So, the timing of the call couldn't be better. And the euphoria of the sale went a long way to placate his bruised feelings.

Lawson outlined to Powers that he would fly down after the shipment arrived, train the maintenance staff and then oversee the installation. And in between, he would get in a few days of fishing.

He explained, "The timing is perfect. I need to get away, particularly with the stress of this serious cash flow shortfall. Plus, everything else we're dealing with."

Although Powers was pleased with the order, he recognized the irony of Lawson's need to go on vacation to relieve his stress. He mused, *how would Lawson, who was financially set for life, handle my frightening situation right about now?*

6

Untimely Death
January, 1991, San Bernardino, CA

Sitting in his law office, Harold Payne answered his phone. It's 11:15, and it's the first time the phone rang all morning.

"Harold, it's Jaden Smythe returning your call. I know you're looking for a check, but my situation is not good. I don't have money to pay any of my bills, not even my rent."

"Jaden, what are you doing to resolve your financial problems?"

"I'm making sales calls to new prospects, trying to get a few projects going. But even if I get some orders, it takes time to complete the work, collect the money and start to pay down my debts."

"Look Jaden, that's not a plan. That's a Hail Mary pass. You sit down and look at your business and figure out how you can shake some money out of the trees. And then call me back with a real plan."

Frustrated, Payne placed an outbound call to another client, one with a six-month past due balance. "Hi, I'd like to speak to Mr. Hearst. Is he in?"

"Who's calling, please?"

"Harold Payne, his attorney."

"Just a second, let me check." After a pause "Sorry, Mr. Hearst is in conference and can't come to the phone right now. Can I take a message?"

Payne did not react well to that tired excuse. And his response was, "Listen, sweetheart. You tell your useless, deadbeat boss to get me a check this week, or I'll shut down his company! And that's no idle threat." With that, he hung up.

Payne sat in his gloomy office and looked around in disgust. His battered, oversize desk was stacked with client files, and there were more all over the floor. But despite the clutter, his pens were lined up next to the blotter, and his yellow legal pad was exactly square to the edge of the desk. What was he doing in this decrepit place? He knew the current recession was not the cause of his problems.

It was his own flawed decision that brought him down. He had come a long way from the heady days as a power attorney with one of LA's largest firms. He was earning mid-six figures in those days, but he made a crucial mistake.

A client whom he despised had called to ask him to backdate a document that would result in a huge windfall for the client. He offered Payne a $100,000 under-the-table cash payment for the illegal transaction. Payne, in a greedy moment of weakness, had his secretary prepare the necessary papers, which he hand-delivered to the client for signature. He was certain the client would eventually get caught for the bogus transaction, but he had made certain that his fingerprints were not on the doctored file.

And sure enough, a year later, the client got caught and slapped with a criminal charge. The managing partner of the law firm, suspecting Payne's involvement, researched and learned the truth. Instead of disbarment, the firm had negotiated a quiet settlement, terminating Payne with no severance or claim to accumulated benefits. Plus, he lost his partnership equity.

And now, Payne worked from this depressing office with dust-covered, second-hand furniture and no staff except a part-time secretary. He was embarrassed by the dismal look and feel of the place, so he always tried to see clients at their office. To encourage that, he used the slogan, *The Attorney Who Makes House Calls.*

Sitting there in a funk, the phone startled him.

"Mr. Payne, this is Martha Billings. My husband is Edward Billings."

"Yes, of course. How are you, Mrs. Billings?"

"Right now, dreadful. My husband passed in his sleep last night." She stopped speaking and sobbed.

"Oh, I am so sorry for your loss. What terrible news."

Regaining her composure, she continued, "Mr. Payne, I need your help, particularly with the business. I am all alone. Can you help me?"

"Absolutely, Mrs. Billings. Did you make any funeral arrangements yet?"

"I called the funeral home in my neighborhood. I have to go there tomorrow morning to decide all the arrangements. Is there any chance you could come with me? I don't know where to begin."

"You're too distraught to make decisions under these circumstances. I'd be glad to go with you. I have your home address. How about I pick you up tomorrow at 9:30?"

When Payne arrived, Martha answered the door wearing a simple dark blue dress that hid her well-rounded curves. She was five foot, four inches, 140 pounds. She wore a little makeup, but it did nothing to cover her reddened, swollen eyes. And graying roots were showing through her brunette hair.

He remembered her as an attractive woman of medium height with a quiet bearing. Her large breasts and shapely legs always stood out in his mind. But her posture and attire played down her looks and her full-figured shape. At first glance, you would describe her as *plain.*

The Cape Cod house was in need of fresh paint in a neighborhood in the $200,000 price range. When Payne entered, he noticed the inexpensive furniture, and the dearth of wall hangings and decorative accessories. It was a clear sign that Billings' business was not throwing off much profit.

The funeral home bore the same appearance as the rest of the lower-income neighborhood. It needed a fresh coat of

24

paint and some new furniture. The owner greeted them with his practiced air of sympathy and compassion. He held Martha's hand as she struggled to maintain her composure.

As the director discussed funeral options, Payne inserted himself into the conversation. He pressed for an inexpensive coffin, a one-day private wake, a brief church service, and burial in their family plot. His head-on, no-nonsense approach saved Martha at least $10,000. And expecting that she had little or no savings, this was huge.

When the arrangements were complete, Payne took her to lunch at a quiet restaurant. He urged her to have a calming glass of wine. She explained that the company had been founded by her husband's only relative, an uncle who had hired Ed to be the sales rep for the firm. The senior Billings was in poor health and wanted the business to survive and remain in the family. He had a small staff of loyal employees, a few who had worked for him for decades. He wanted Ed to take over the company, keeping it intact after his death.

The battery distribution warehouse was never a thriving success, as the uncle vigilantly avoided risks. When wholesalers and retailers were moving away from the pricing directives dictated by manufacturers, he continued selling everything at full wholesale price.

When he died unexpectedly, Ed took over the reins with no real business acumen. He ran the operation exactly as his uncle did, making no changes. As expected, the firm continued to falter, with Ed doing everything he could to keep the staff employed.

Martha recognized she knew almost nothing about their business, other than it had been losing money. She questioned Payne about selling the company, despite its weak financial position.

Payne responded, "I'll move my schedule around to spend a few days there. I can review the books and I'll talk to some of the customers and vendors. Then I'll advise you on possibly selling the business."

"Possibly sell it?" she asked.

He ignored her painful question and his answer.

Payne asked where she worked, which was as an on-call substitute teacher. He told her to phone her school and explain her circumstances, as she would be unavailable for teaching until the week after the burial. Payne also instructed her to go to her husband's office for a short time every day, and tell the staff to continue to manage the daily operation.

As he spoke, Martha's fear subsided. She also felt relieved and grateful for his compassion and take-charge attitude, and his willingness to help her. But the fear of living without her husband would not go away.

7

Dispensing Business Advice

The next day at 9:30, Payne got a call from Andy Hearst. Before Payne could thank him for returning his call, an angry Hearst jumped in. "Harold, what's this shit about shutting me down? Don't you know we're in a recession? I'm scrambling to hold things together and you threaten me? I need your help, not your bluster."

"Sorry, Andy. I was reacting to your secretary's lame line about 'being in conference'. Train her to be honest, and you'll get better cooperation from your creditors. So what kind of help do you need?"

"I'm having trouble collecting money from my customers. No one has any cash."

"Shit, that's easy. I'll come to your office this afternoon and see what I can do. Trust me, I'll get you some money quickly. See you later."

Payne's next call was from Jaden Smythe. "Mr. Payne, I sent over a basic plan, and put down a few ideas, but it's not organized. Did you look at it?"

"Jaden, I read it over, and your problem is working with the builders. You need to sell to consumers and get full price for your work. I'm having one of my clients call you. He has a small ad agency, and can help you reach the homeowners in this area and get some sales. And then you get me some money!"

"Great! I'll wait for his call. And I promise, I'll get a payment to you right away."

That afternoon, Payne went to Andy Hearst's office and reviewed his accounts receivable. He was appalled by the amounts and aging of the debts. He started with the oldest bills and began calling the customers.

Payne introduced himself as the company's attorney and politely told them he was instructed to file suit if they didn't agree to a payment schedule. Within two hours, he had commitments for tens of thousands of dollars. Making a list of all the promises, he drafted a letter to them, confirming their payment schedule.

Payne then met with Hearst and updated him on his progress, handing him the list and the draft. He gave him specific instructions. "Personalize this letter and send it to the CEO of every one of your clients and follow the terms exactly. It will end your collection problems. Do the same with any new customers."

"You did all that in a couple of hours? That's fantastic!"

"I'm only going to bill you three hours for today. And over the next 30 days, I want you to get my invoices current from the money you will now collect. And I expect you to stay current going forward. Are we clear?"

"Harold, I can't thank you enough. I'm not good at dunning people for money. What you just did would take me a week, and with far less success."

"That's because you don't know how to talk to people, you dumb shit. You don't wear your sales hat when you're trying to collect money. Business is not about getting sales, it's about getting paid."

8

The Funeral

The next morning Payne, dressed in a navy-blue tailored suit and a dated Brioni tie, picked up Martha, and drove to the funeral home. She was wearing a black dress and low heels. Her better-applied makeup helped cover her blotched skin. She was looking much more attractive today. Even her hair was better coiffed.

They followed the hearse to the church in his car, and then to the cemetery. A few of Martha's distant relatives, who barely knew her, came in from out of town, resentful of having to make the trip. All nine company employees filled the mourners.

The ceremony at the cemetery was brief. The minister read a short eulogy, said some prayers and the body was interred. And after the cheerless hugs, kisses and tears everyone left without a word. Payne offered to take Martha to lunch, knowing she did not want to be home alone after the funeral.

At the restaurant, he again suggested she have a glass of wine, although she was emotionally in a better place than she was earlier in the week. They ate without much conversation and as Martha relaxed, the dialogue picked up.

She told Payne that she had been thinking about the company. "I feel like I have no choice but to sell it. My key concern is that I know nothing about the business."

"You should wait a while, before you do anything drastic. Your financial future is at stake here."

"But it's losing money. I'm scared."

"When I come in to look at the books, I'll try to determine its worth. I'll also see if there's any way to quickly increase sales quickly to add value to the company. Then you can make an informed decision on which way to go."

Reaching across the table, Martha pressed his forearm, and trembling she responded, "Harold, you have been so kind. This business is all I have, and I'm afraid it's worthless. If I could get even a little money from the business, it would be a godsend."

Payne could see the fear in her eyes, and he calmed her down by saying, "I'll squeeze some amount of cash from that business. Let's meet at the office next Tuesday. We can check out the books and the entire operation."

His reassuring words helped her relax, yet she was still frightened. How could Ed let his life insurance policy lapse? Her part-time job earned only a couple of hundred dollars a week. Her mortgage alone was $1,200. How was she going to eat? Pay bills?

She couldn't imagine how Payne could save her. "Oh, Harold. I can't wait until Tuesday comes."

9

A Plan Emerges

The following week, Harold Payne went to Billings' office and met with Martha. He sat there gazing at her, recognizing how the strain of her husband's loss was affecting her looks. The makeup she wore did little to hide the effects of the crying. Yet, despite that, he still found her attractive and felt compassion for the struggle she was enduring.

As they sipped coffee in the small conference room, he wanted to reach out and hug her, sensing that she anxiously needed to be held. The feeling passed as they got into the reason they were there.

Payne scanned a file of papers and Martha said, "I can't be much help. My husband shared none of the details, except it is losing money. Running it is beyond my ability. I should just try to sell it right away before it loses more money."

"First let's see if it has any equity. If not, selling it would not provide you any funds. Please relax. I am here to help you so you're not stressed."

Payne spent the next couple of hours combing the books, calling the bank to confirm balances, and walking through the warehouse, checking the stock. With each step, he told her of his findings, and all of it was discouraging. After a few hours of this, Martha couldn't take it any longer and left. He told her he would stay longer and see what else he could uncover, and he would call her later.

When he finished reviewing the books, which were in terrible shape, Payne got on the phone and called all the vendors and the battery manufacturers. He introduced himself as the attorney for the firm and told them of Billings' passing. None of them took the news well, as they all had money due to them. He explained that he was reviewing the books and would be back to them with a plan shortly.

Payne then phoned the largest customers to learn about how they felt about doing business with the company. A few had strong relationships with Billings and were open to discussing the situation with him. They all had the same message. With the recession-driven economy, sales were sluggish, and they were all looking for an edge to maintain volume. Some more competitive distributors were offering them promotions and deals, but Billings was reluctant to cut prices. When Payne asked if they would make more purchases if prices were lower, they all said they would welcome that change.

Payne spent another hour sitting in Billings' drab office pondering the situation. The firm had no value, and selling it was out of the question. A plan to salvage the company emerged. He called Martha and asked her to meet at a restaurant near her home, as he had some ideas how they might save the company.

When she arrived, Payne was at the bar, drinking Chivas Regal on the rocks. She looked noticeably better. Her complexion had cleared, and even her posture was better. As she approached, he could see her large breasts pushing against the fabric of her cream knit dress, which sent a bolt through his loins. She chose a Manhattan and was eager to hear what he had to say.

Payne told her about all the calls and how those conversations helped him develop his plan. He also shared his finding: the company has no value. Finishing their drinks, they moved to a table where they ordered dinner. Payne outlined his plan.

"I'm going to call a meeting of all the largest vendors and battery manufacturers. When I offer them a plan to recover their money over time, they will participate."

"But how can you be sure?"

"Because they'll prefer my alternative, rather than have the company go bankrupt."

"I'm still skeptical, but continue."

"My next step will be to offer a deep discount on all the product in inventory, and follow up with smaller discounts on future orders. This will generate cash flow, but not a long-term solution. It will stabilize the company and allow us to move forward."

Payne then explained his recovery strategy for the company and make it grow. He would take the reins and go out, open new accounts and make sales. And if the plan was successful, he would hire a sales rep to expand the customer base. Then, they could decide if she should hire a CEO or sell the company.

Martha sat there stunned. "How could you afford to spend that amount of time on my business? It's an exciting idea, but it can't work."

"Look, let me be honest. The lawyer business has not been great, and I'm burned out. Besides, I'm excited about this challenge. I've been helping a couple of other clients with their business, and I have a knack for turning fortunes around."

"But how can I possibly pay you?

"Don't worry about paying me right now. Let's save your company, and then you can compensate me. I have a good feeling about making this work."

At that point, Martha's demeanor changed. She smiled for the first time in a long while, and her whole body seemed to relax. She drained her wine, and he poured her another one.

When they had finished their dinner and wine, they left the restaurant, and Payne walked her to her car. She reached up and kissed him on the cheek. "Thank you for all you're doing for me. I've been so lost, and now you've given me hope." She drove off, feeling better than she had in months.

Payne stood in the parking lot, watching her leave. As he walked to his car, he was sensing the exhilaration this new challenge would bring to his tedious existence.

10

Securing Reluctant Commitments

The creditor meeting began at 5 pm, two months to the day after Billings' funeral. Payne insisted Martha attend. She wore a simple black dress, minimal makeup, and little jewelry. He was certain that her presence would add a sympathy factor to the meeting.

About 20 creditors came to the company's office, where Payne had set up makeshift meeting space in the warehouse using rented folding chairs. He did this intentionally, as he didn't want them to get too comfortable. Payne also thought they would respond better to a simple office setting rather than a restaurant or hotel meeting room.

He opened the gathering by introducing Martha as the widow of the deceased CEO, and himself as the firm's lawyer. He then provided a snapshot of the company's finances, debts, inventory and other pertinent data. The assessment was a sobering revelation, although not unexpected.

The VP of one of the battery manufacturers commented. "Mr. Payne, this sounds pretty grim. How can you possibly turn this around?"

"I have a plan. It's solid, but it will require the full cooperation of everyone in this room."

Payne then presented his solution to avoid bankruptcy. He saw a few of the smaller vendors were nervous, but they all sat at rapt attention. He explained how he planned to move the current inventory to raise some cash to remain solvent. His plan called for a sales program focused on opening new clients with an aggressive pricing plan. This had not been done in the past.

Payne explained. "I polled the customer base and they were very receptive to the idea. They all said, with discount pricing, they would increase purchases. I can use the same strategy to get some new accounts."

To make the plan work, he required a new set of payment terms from all the vendors. And this was the hard part. The entire block of payables would be held in abeyance for three months while he would pay new orders COD.

He assured them, "I will take no fees for my services during this time, and Mrs. Billings would draw a minimal salary, the same as her husband had drawn, which is just enough for her to survive. The caveat, however, is everyone must agree, or I will have to shutter this company immediately."

The drastic step would certainly mean bankruptcy, and none of them would get paid for the monies owed. In closing, Payne told them, "I must have a decision in 24 hours, as time is the enemy of this rescue plan."

The 14 smaller creditors all gave their tacit approval on the spot, with the remaining the larger creditors saying they would respond the next day. One of the small creditors said, "I've been working with the Billings since they opened their doors. They're good people and I want to see this firm survive."

The following morning, with Martha in tow, wearing the same outfit as the previous evening, he went to the bank. Knowing he was exaggerating the results to revive the company, the lending officer agreed to only a small increase in their line of credit.

They left the bank smiling, as Martha said, "I cannot believe what you just did. I loved the way you handled the meeting, but wasn't it sort of dishonest?"

"It's going to take a massive effort, a lot of luck, and more than a little deception to turn this ship around. And frankly, I'm not completely sure I can pull it off."

"But it still seems deceptive."

"If I have to lie, cheat and steal to save your company, I'm going to do it. Now, forget I just said that, and trust me to take the right steps. Now, let me get to the office and sell those deals we told him we already have on the books. And I'll follow up with the few vendors who have not committed."

By the end of the day, Payne had made a few sales, and he sat with Martha and told her about his successes on the phone. Reassuring her, he said he was feeling confident that they would pull this off and revive the firm. It was then that the time was right to broach the important subject of how he would manage the operation, and what he would expect as compensation.

"I've been thinking about what we need to succeed. And I've also thought about how I will be paid. Since you have no experience in running a business, and no management skills that could help us now, I'm going to take over as interim CEO. I will be in charge and make all the decisions. Are you okay with that?"

"Of course. I'm in no position to run the company. But I do want to know what's going on."

"I will meet with you regularly and keep you informed. I'll cut any unnecessary overhead and operating costs. As I told the creditors and the bank, I'll take no compensation until we're profitable. When the company can afford it, I'll draw a fee of $1,500 per week. Each quarter, if the company is profitable, I'll get a 20% bonus, and the rest will be yours to draw down as cash flow allows. For me, it's all performance related, so you have no risk in the event I'm not productive."

"It certainly sounds fair."

"You will continue to take the same amount Ed had been getting. And it will increase to the same amount as me when I start to draw my fees. Does it sound okay to you? If you agree, I'll put it in writing with a simple agreement."

"Harold, as you know, I have no business experience, so I have to rely on your judgment. What you have outlined strikes me as fair. And yes, I would like the comfort of having it in writing."

"You won't be sorry, Martha. You once mentioned to me you were a substitute teacher. Is there any chance you could get a full-time position, which would give you benefits? It would save on health care insurance. It would also increase your income and allow you to live a little more comfortably that much sooner."

"Yes, now my life has changed so drastically. I need to be more productive and occupied during the day. I'll look into it." And just saying that made her realize that she would now be unbound from her household duties, and free to broaden her life. Being around someone like Harold would expand her horizons.

11

Strategy Shortcomings

Two weeks later, Harold Payne was sitting in his new office at the battery company when he got a call from his law client Will, who owned the ad agency, "Hi Harold. I tracked you down to thank you for recommending your client, Jaden Smythe to me. He hired me to put together an ad campaign and I think it will bring him a ton of business.

"Your secretary told me you were helping another client turn their company around. Can I be of any service to you?"

"Thanks, Will, but this is a sales-driven project. And advertising just isn't the right approach."

"Harold, how can you say that? Advertising drives sales. It would probably cut your selling cycle in half."

"I'll be honest with you, Will. I'm not a big believer in any kind of marketing, except in retail, like with Jaden's firm. I'm a strong salesman, so I know I can get the job done without the expense of a campaign."

Will was taken aback by Payne's ill-informed comments. He realized Payne knew nothing about marketing, but he also recognized he was not open to being educated on its benefits. But he wondered how successful Payne could be in helping clients with their business if he didn't understand the critical role of marketing. He politely responded, "Okay, whatever you say. But, I'm here if you need me."

Payne sat at the desk with a self-satisfied smile on his face. He was gloating at the number of sales he brought in, just with phone calls. And, he sold the entire group of creditors on his restructuring. And now he was about to go on the road and open some new accounts. "Who needs marketing?" he said aloud.

His sense of accomplishment was bolstered by the other two clients from his law practice whom he had helped, and who were already paying down the past due money they owed him. Billings Battery Company was by far his biggest challenge, but he was confident with his sales drive, he would be successful. Payne grew convinced that he had a real feel for turning around troubled companies. And he recognized that there was an opportunity to capitalize on this newfound talent in a big way.

But did he have a special skill? Was he capable of overcoming this enormous challenge?

12

Ignoring Boundaries

Returning from a successful road trip, Payne called Martha as soon as he got to the office. "I'm back in town and I can't wait to tell you about my great trip. It was far beyond expectations. I want to celebrate with you tonight. How about I take you to a special restaurant? So, dress up, and I'll pick you up at 7."

Hearing the excitement in his voice, she responded, "Oh, Harold, I can't wait to hear about it. And I have good news to tell you when we meet." When she hung up, she felt alive. And she realized just how deep her depression went. She hadn't been on a *date* in years, not even with her husband. And this felt like a date.

Their struggling business had driven a wedge between her and Ed, as he had a difficult time coping with a company relentlessly bleeding money. Their sex life and even their affection for each other evaporated, and they often fought about being unable to pay their bills.

Her part-time teaching job had not brought in much income, and she was too depressed to look for a better job. And Ed had always been demanding and very strict about the cleanliness of their house and having his dinner ready when he got home. He was old fashioned, even when he couldn't support them. Many factors contributed to her despair, and now everything was changing.

Maybe Harold really could rescue the company. And maybe she could enjoy some financial security. But for now, she had to get ready for her dinner with him. She quickly made appointments with her hairdresser and nail salon, and

41

then went through her wardrobe to decide what to wear. The euphoria and the *special occasion* preparation were making her giddy.

After his call, Payne sat in his office reacting to Martha's delighted response. He missed hearing her voice, and was hoping tonight she would wear something showing off those large breasts and hips she kept hidden under those baggy dresses.

He was feeling excited about his accomplishments over the last couple of months. By using generous initial-order deals and lots of bluster, he had opened a few very large accounts. And he expected more would respond to his deals over the next few weeks. Despite the reduced profit margins, he was sensing the potential with this small company.

Payne showed up at exactly 7, and he had a bouquet with him. Appraising her, he commented, "You look beautiful! And I brought some beautiful flowers to match your looks." Despite the cliché, she was flattered.

As with hair and nails, Martha spent a lot of time selecting just the right dress, shoes and jewelry. And she even wore her best lingerie. She was not expecting him to see her underwear. Just wearing it made her feel more like a woman. Although she wanted him to see her as attractive, she had no intention of dressing to seduce him.

He took her to Spaggi's Restaurant in Upland, a high-end eatery, where she had never been. It was a striking contemporary building that made you want to see inside.

Martha sat there in awe of the beauty of the interior décor while she sipped her Manhattan. As he drank his martini, Payne told her about his trip and the new accounts he opened. He explained, "These are much bigger companies than our current list of customers. And because of this, Billings Battery is growing, and more notably it will be profitable!"

"It's so exciting. I can't believe that you are actually making this happen. I would never have thought it possible."

"Honey, this is why I told you to wait before you went ahead and tried to sell the company. Now you will have so many more options."

Payne suggested the evening's dinner special, Chateaubriand for Two. Martha blanched at the $80 cost, but he smiled. "It's a special night. And you deserve something special."

With their dinner entrees, Payne ordered an expensive bottle of Barolo, a wine Martha had never tasted. As they finished the wine, he asked about her good news. In the excitement, she forgot to tell him about her new position. She had gone to the principal of the school where she taught, and inquired about a full-time teaching position.

The principal was delighted. "Of course, I can accommodate you. You are so very well-liked here by both the students and the faculty. I never knew you wanted to move up to full-time. Can you start right away?"

"That's great news. Things are really starting to look up for you."

Martha invited him back for coffee at her place. She placed demitasse and pastries on the coffee table and sat next to him on the couch. They were both feeling the effects of the drinks and wine, adding to the exhilaration of their good news.

Martha, sitting close to Payne, bumped knees as she served the coffee. She wanted him to give her a sign it was okay, but he seemed to ignore it. She hungered for some affection and hoped he would just hold her.

Sensing this, Payne made a more overt move with his knee, testing her. He then took her hand, pulled her to him and kissed her. She responded hungrily, sliding closer to him. In a typical clumsy move, he grabbed her right breast and began fondling it, aroused by its heft and firmness.

That's all it took. After a few minutes of this kissing and groping, Martha stood up and walked him into the bedroom where she undressed down to her underwear and quickly slipped under the covers. He stripped down to his white

43

shorts and black socks. As he got into bed, he admired her full but exquisite shape with its flat, smooth abdomen.

Lying there, she hastily removed his briefs, while he slid off her lingerie. She quickly became aroused and rolled over on top of him. In less than a minute, she reached a full orgasm, but kept moving until his ejaculation. When she rolled off him, he ran into the bathroom and cleaned himself off. When he returned to bed, she sobbed. "I'm so sorry but I couldn't help myself. You have no idea what my life has been like for so long. I can't remember when Ed and I last made love. Please don't think I'm horrible."

"Honey, you have nothing to apologize for. I'm the one who initiated this. You simply reacted out of need."

"Harold, there's no question that my body was desperate for sex, but I should still have more control. And then my instantly quick orgasm was so embarrassing. I don't think I could ever look at you again."

Payne put his arms around her and pulled her in close. He held her for what seemed like hours, kissing her forehead, and lightly stroking her legs, abdomen and breasts. They both grew aroused again, but the second time they made love, it was far slower and more intimate. After again running to the bathroom, he returned and lay in bed with her for a while more. He then got up and got dressed, telling Martha he had to leave.

She asked, "When will I see you again?"

"It will be soon, I promise. I'll call you in the morning."

Martha lay awake for hours after Payne left. She was bombarded with conflicting emotions and confusion in her mind.

On one hand, she was deeply troubled she had betrayed Ed so soon after his untimely death. But why her feelings of betrayal? Hadn't he ignored her need for intimacy without even some small sign of attention? Being with Payne exposed the chasm in their marriage.

Martha was also embarrassed by her forward moves to let Payne know that she wanted his affection, even just to be

44

held. But once he got her vibe, he rushed forward with his somewhat clumsy approach. She realized that he also felt awkward stepping into this first foray at intimacy with her.

Reliving the experience, she was again mortified by her display of wanton sexual hunger. Despite these conflicts, it ended up being an exciting, sexually-charged interlude, something she sorely missed. She also felt guilty by her underlying hope that it would continue and grow into something more. But should she be encouraging a relationship with someone who was running her company?

13

Filling Needs

At the office early the next morning, Harold Payne was looking for ways to reduce costs and make the company function more efficiently. He had previously recognized the bookkeeper was too error-prone to keep. And he realized with better systems and records, the firm could function without the warehouse manager. He called each of them into his office and terminated them with a small severance package.

Payne then called a woman who was a former client of his a few years back. Christie Lang had been the office manager for a local manufacturing company for four years when she was caught embezzling money from the firm. It was a small indiscretion triggered by a need to help her dying mother. However, she knew it was wrong and was contrite with her irresponsible decision. Payne had represented her and arranged for her charges to be dropped if she made restitution. This avoided a messy trial, but it meant she would have a difficult time finding a managerial position without a referral. As a result, she took a job as a bartender at a restaurant, where they didn't do much of a background check.

Payne met her after work at the office. Christie was rail thin with bleached blonde hair matching her shape. She wore more makeup than she needed as she had a pretty face with striking blue eyes. She was attractive but had a hard look about her. Eyeing her, Payne thought that she needed a good meal to help put a little weight on her bones.

He explained the firm's business but before he offered her the bookkeeper position, he admonished her. "Look, Christie. I know your history, and I'm willing to give you a break, but you must promise me you won't repeat the mistake you made the last time."

"Mr. Payne, I will always be grateful for what you did for me and would never do anything to hurt you. It was too painful a lesson to ever make a mistake like that again.

"I would love to work for you, but my hours need to be flexible so I can bartend part-time. I'm still paying back the money."

"We can set hours that fit your schedule. And call me Harold."

Christie started the next day and reorganized the books in a professional way.

That afternoon Martha called. "I thought you were going to call me yesterday morning?"

"I'm so sorry. It's been very hectic. I have been working from early morning into the night. How about if I come over this evening, and bring takeout dinner?"

"Sounds delightful. I can't wait to see you."

Payne showed up at 7:30 with two deli platters of roast turkey and two servings of cheesecake. He also brought a bottle of pinot noir. They wolfed down the dinner and gulped down the wine.

Then it was a footrace into the bedroom for a sexual escapade lasting nearly four hours. It would have gone on longer, but Payne ran out of gas. Martha paced herself much slower and he let her direct him. When they were done, they showered together, giving her the idea he might stay over this time. He once again told her he had to leave. She suggested he bring some toiletries and extra clothes to keep at her house, so he could spend overnights with her. She told him she was very lonely, particularly at night, and found it difficult to sleep alone.

47

"Let me think about it. I don't want to rush into anything. And the last thing I want to do is to hurt you in any way."

Having gotten her hopes up, Martha carefully concealed the deep disappointment she was feeling. After he left, she lay in bed, yearning for the warmth of a man sleeping next to her. Why didn't Harold get that? She was determined to win him over and make him understand a woman's basic need was so much more important than the physical sex.

14

The First Bone Yard Candidate

For the next week, Harold Payne spent nearly every night with Martha before leaving for another long road trip. As with all his previous rendezvous, he came over for drinks and sex and then left. This troubled Martha, as she realized his behavior grew more indifferent and uncaring.

She was becoming disappointed her aspirations of a deeper liaison with him were not being fulfilled. He could not appease her need for loving companionship and affection, except for the sexual intimacy. He was not a warm person, and was apparently interested mostly in the physical side of the equation.

Martha had hoped the sexual relationship would win over his feelings, but recognized it was purely carnal. She decided she would have to confront this problem when he returned from his business trip.

Payne arrived a couple of days earlier than scheduled and spent long hours at the office. He excitedly told Christie about all the new accounts he opened. The first day back, he had a working lunch meeting with her to discuss the staffing. Over sandwiches and coffee, she provided her ideas about restructuring the responsibilities of the workers.

While Payne was out of town, Christie had been working on a plan to streamline the administrative processes. "Harold, if I can buy a new computer to replace this piece of junk in the office and get some upgraded software, I can eliminate most of the staff."

"Buy the computer. I appreciate someone with initiative."

"This operation is much easier than running a manufacturing plant. With spreadsheets, I can handle the purchasing and inventory. And with a couple of low-skilled workers, I can oversee the logistics."

"I agree. Do all of it. We can save a bundle on overhead."

She told him about the inventory manager's screw-up of a big new customer's order. "They sent four pallets of the wrong batteries out on a rush-order basis. They had to be retrieved, and the replacement order shipped by special truck. This fiasco cost far more than the profit on the entire order."

Payne was furious. The manager had been with the firm before Ed's passing. And Payne was looking for a reason to let him go. Payne called him into his office.

"Juan, how long have you been working here?"

"Señor Payne, I have been here eleven years, from the beginning with Señor Ed and his uncle, Joseph." He made the sign of the cross as he mentioned his deceased employers.

"Well, if you've been here so long, how could you fuck up an order like you did?"

"No, no. I didn't make mistake. The wrong product code was on purchase order."

"You did make the mistake. You should have questioned it, you dumb fucking Spick!"

"That's no my job. I go by what on order."

"That's no your job? Well, now you have no job. So, get the fuck out of here. You're fired!"

Payne had deliberately left the office door open to broadcast his tirade against Juan. The receptionist acted like she didn't hear anything, as Christie sat in her office and took in every demeaning word. She was disturbed by Payne's harsh treatment, but took it as a lesson on what to expect and how to deal with him in the future.

When Payne did not call Martha following his expected return, she called him, "When did you get back Harold? I had been hoping to hear from you."

"Hi Martha, honey. I got back a couple of days ago, but I have so much catching up to do I can't get to see you for a few days. This place doesn't seem to function properly when I'm not here."

"Well, I need to see you. I want to talk. When can you come over?"

Payne sensed Martha's chilly attitude. He delayed their meeting. "I'll make it the day after tomorrow, but it will be late. I've been putting in 16-hour days."

"Okay, see you then."

Hanging up, he knew what was coming.

15

Discomforting Rejection

Harold Payne had been in town for five days and could have met with Martha on any of those evenings. But he put it off each day because he didn't want to face the consequences. So, on the sixth night, he'd get it over with. He showed up at 9:30.

Martha was dressed in a baggy sweater and jeans, no makeup, and did not look like she was expecting a visit from a lover. Payne got the message, and although he really would like to have gotten in bed with her, he refrained.

They sat on opposite sides of the couch. Martha started the conversation, "I cannot continue doing this, this charade, this tryst. It's humiliating. I enjoy the sex with you, but it can't be just sex. I'm not that kind of woman. I need more, and you frankly can't give it to me. We just have to stop."

"I'm sorry. I never meant for this to happen. And you're right. I'm too distracted, and I cannot be in a love relationship right now. But I am the caretaker of your business, and it is about to become wildly successful. We'll continue to meet, but it will be strictly on a professional level, I promise."

Martha was uncomfortable in his presence after everything that she had experienced. She knew it would be impossible to have just a business relationship with him. "Well, that is certainly good news. If what you say comes to fruition, I can sell the company that much sooner. And believe me, it can't come soon enough."

Payne was disappointed. He enjoyed this new venture, and he was not looking for it to end. Besides, the big money was about to start rolling in. He told her he would keep her informed of any new developments, and he stood to leave.

After letting him out and locking the door, Martha went back and sat on the sofa, reflecting on their brief exchange. While she didn't expect the confrontation to be any different, she was still disappointed in the outcome. Somehow, she hoped that he would have had a change of heart. She knew better. His news about the company's outlook was encouraging, but it did nothing to improve her mood.

She accepted her loneliness would not be overcome with her hoped-for relationship with Payne. She sobbed. After a good cry, she retreated to bed, determined to control her own destiny.

As Payne drove home, he thought about their talk, and although he expected exactly what happened, he was angry because it didn't have to be this way. Why couldn't they have a sexual relationship? He treated her with respect, not like a whore. He knew she needed the intimacy, and he was there to provide it. And he was so good at it she obviously she enjoyed it, just as he did.

He was going to miss lusting over her body, especially those firm tits and ass. Why couldn't she act like an adult? He was certain that in a week or two, she would call him when her sexual needs were aroused and want to be with him again. He knew he had that ability to make a woman crave the sexual intensity that he brought to the bedroom.

He'd sit back and wait for her call.

16

A Woman's Scorn

Payne scheduled a meeting with Christie to talk about the company's status. She explained that the warehouse and shipping were running more smoothly after the restructure, driving profits up substantially.

He shared his projection with her. "Sales are going to escalate much faster than before. In fact, I'm going to talk to the building owner about increasing the warehouse space."

"Good idea. We're bulging at the seams now."

With the next-door tenant gone, he was certain he could renegotiate a new lease for the entire building at a much better rate.

When she handed him the cash flow report, he was shocked. The company had gone from annual sales of less than $1 million and losing upwards of $100,000 last year to making several hundred thousand dollars profit in a few short months. Sales would soon reach more than a million a month with a much lower payroll.

He instructed Christie to pay the line of credit down to zero for the time being, and he would tell her when to draw again. He told her to increase his salary to $2,000 per week and do the same for Martha. He also had her write a bonus check to Martha for $50,000.

Christie nodded. She was nervous about pulling all that cash out of the account. Recognizing that she was apprehensive, he told her, "I know what I'm doing so not to worry. We can draw down on the credit line again if we need it."

He also advised her that a new customer was coming to the office at noon for a meeting and a tour of the facility.

At 12:30, Martha unexpectedly walked into the office and was shocked that it was nearly empty. With no one at the front desk, she walked further into the office, and seeing only Christie, who she didn't know, asked, "Who are you? And where is everybody?"

Before she could answer, Martha went through the warehouse door and did not recognize any of the few people working there. She raced back into the office and glared at Christie shouting, "Where's Harold!"

"Mr. Payne is in his office, meeting with a customer and has the door closed. And I'm sorry, but I don't know who you are?"

Without answering, Martha charged into Payne's office. He looked up, surprised. "Martha, what are you doing here? You can't just show up. This is a business we're running, and I'm in a conference with our important new client. So please call me later, and we can talk, or even meet if you'd like."

"Where are all my employees? Where are the people who worked for my husband? What have you done with them?"

"I can't talk to you now. We can discuss this later."

"I want answers now. What happened to all those loyal people who worked for Ed? God, I hope you didn't fire them."

"Yes, we had to lay off certain staff members who were not performing, or who we couldn't keep busy. It wasn't an easy decision, but they were costing you money. You're the one who's going to benefit from this."

"My God! You had no right to do that. I own this company, and you did this terrible thing without even asking me first. That is unacceptable and outrageous!"

"Martha, it is your company, but you put me in charge. And we have a written contract. I certainly don't have to ask your permission to take any necessary steps to ensure that we are successful. It's why you hired me."

"Well, you can bet that I'm also going to fire you. And where is my copy of the signed agreement? You never gave it to me. I'm going to hire another lawyer, and I'm going to sell the company or find a new CEO, one who will respect my position. You can expect to be out of here in the next month."

The client sat there stunned by the exchange. It was very uncomfortable to see this emotional woman ranting and skewering Payne.

Moving to the door, Payne said to her, "When I finish my meeting, I will locate the agreement and drop off your copy. Be sure to read it carefully. There is a three-month notice clause, plus a penalty for terminating me without cause."

And calling out to Christie, he asked, "Do you have the check ready for Mrs. Billings?"

Christie handed an envelope to Martha, saying, "This was going out in today's mail."

Martha grabbed the envelope and stormed out the door. When she got in her car, she opened it and was shocked. Driving away, she realized how foolish she had been. She knew she did not act like a mature business owner, but a hysterical housewife.

Closing the door, Payne apologized to his prospect. "I'm so sorry for that intrusion, but she lost her husband several months ago and is still suffering. And she just doesn't understand business."

"Oh, I'm sorry. I could see how troubled she is."

"Wait till she sees just how big that check is. Her eyes will bulge and she will have an epiphany. She will change her mind about terminating me by tomorrow."

As he was describing this, he could see that this new prospect would never become a client. Martha's angry scene had closed that door forever. He wasted all that time cultivating this client.

After the prospect left, Payne sat there seething, as he thought about what he had just witnessed. *How could she barge in here and embarrass me like that in front of one of the biggest clients we'll ever land? And where's the appreciation for all I've done for her? I rescued her bankrupt company, and I'm getting her more money than she's ever seen in her life. I even satisfied her needs with sex like she's never had before. And now she wants to fire me? What's her fucking problem?*

As he calmed down, he pulled out the two copies of the signed agreement, and reread the entire document. He then pulled up the file on his computer and went to the page with the bonus clause. He located the sentence that read, *If the company is profitable in any quarter, the CEO will earn a bonus of 20% of the profit.* He changed the last word from *profit* to *sales.*

The one-word edit made a huge difference in the amount of his bonus. Printing two copies of just that page, he replaced them with the original copies, and put one set in an envelope for Martha. He took the other copy home.

He gave Martha's envelope to the receptionist and told her to leave early and drop the envelope off at the address on the front.

17

Change in Plans

Martha's outburst in his office changed everything for Payne. He had been feeling sorry for her and gave her 100% of his effort. But she didn't appreciate it. First, she throws him out of her bedroom, and now she's going to fire him as CEO. He couldn't understand her ingratitude.

If he hadn't come to her aid and rescued the business, she would live in a flophouse somewhere. Deep down, he knew she didn't have a clue about how a business ran, but despite that premonition, he was still surprised and upset at her total rejection of him. Payne just didn't get the connection between the sexual escapades and the business relationship.

Before this new threat, Payne had previously come up with a long-term scheme to skim profits as the company's sales surged. His plan called for him to increase his own income in a clandestinely way that didn't show up on the books.

Martha couldn't grasp the value of his contribution to the firm's success, and the level of compensation that went with it. For that plan to work, she had to receive income she never imagined.

Payne also expected he would arrange for the sale of the company down the road, earning himself a huge retainer. And who knows, possibly stay on as a consultant. But Martha's mindset changed everything.

With this new development, he had to alter his timetable substantially. Instead of the petty larceny scheme he had envisioned, he needed a new plan to make a big strike. His scheme needed time to work. So, must move quickly to avoid being fired before he was ready. He called Diego Santo, The Brazilian.

18

Space to Grow

After the horrific office scene, Payne called the bank. He spoke to the lending officer who had approved the original increase in the company's line of credit. Business was so good that he had paid down the entire loan. He also mentioned that because of the rapid pace of growth, he would need to borrow larger sums of money from time to time.

The banker commented, "I've been watching your activity, and the increases in deposits, and if you need a larger line, I'd approve it. And Mr. Payne, don't hesitate to use the bank for a reference. I'll personally vouch for your creditworthiness."

Next, he called the landlord of his building.

"Hi, this is Harold Payne, CEO of Billings Battery. I'm interested in renting the other half of your building, and under the right terms, I'd sign a twenty-year lease. Needless to say, it would have to be your best square-foot rate. If we strike a deal, I could take the space immediately, as is, without any buildout or broker's commission."

And to ice the deal, he suggested he check the firm's credit with the bank. An hour later, the owner called back, and he got his deal.

He told Christie to order a pizza for the two of them to share during a working lunch meeting. He instructed her to open a new checking account at another bank, and to buy another computer.

He explained, "The company is setting up a second division, and all the sales from some of the newer accounts would go through that subsidiary and through the new checking account."

Payne also gave her a raise of $100 per week and told her to put in expenses for her gas and lunches. Christie was excited. She envisioned where her role could go with all these new developments. And the profits!

19

Added Insurance

A week later, Harold Payne told Christie to call in the company's insurance broker to update the policies.

The agent came a few days later to meet with Payne. After introducing himself as the new CEO, he walked the agent through the newly expanded warehouse. Not having visited the premises in over three years, the broker was impressed with the company's growth.

Returning to his office, he requested the agent review all the company's policies. He wanted to be sure the coverage now reflected the firm's size and included the more than doubling of its inventory. He also wanted to be sure there was adequate coverage for errors and omissions, theft, embezzlement, etc.

He explained that after Billings died, his widow now owned the company. And unfortunately, she didn't have a clue about running a business. Payne wanted to be sure that after his departure, possibly within the year, that Mrs. Billings was properly protected in the event his replacement or anyone else connected to the firm tried to take advantage of her.

The broker thought his foresight was commendable and assured Payne that he would provide the best coverage available.

That evening, after everyone had left the office, Payne thought about his expansion of all the company's insurance policies. Although it would cost an additional $3,000 to $5,000 more a year, he was convinced it was a sound fiscal decision.

Payne also had an ulterior motive. He knew that sometime in the near future, he would have to leave the company prematurely, and he would not be adequately compensated for saving the firm and providing Martha a nest egg to ensure her financial future.

Although his plans were incomplete, he wanted to take what he considered fair, and not destroy the company. The new insurance coverage would provide a financial hedge to keep the company from imploding.

That evening, while still at the office, The Brazilian returned his call.

"Diego, I have a job for you. We need to meet in a couple of weeks at my law office."

20

Poking the Bear

Depositing the check from Harold Payne had given Martha a feeling of security. The entire time she was married, she and her late husband never had that much money in their account. This only added to her conflict. So, before she took any drastic steps, she decided to try one more time to work out an acceptable separation with Payne.

Between the steady paychecks, the bonus, and having lost about 10 pounds, all added to her newfound self-confidence. This, plus her new wardrobe had people giving her appraising looks. She remembered the last time Payne came over, and although she was wearing sweats, he didn't even notice her weight loss. That was the least of his flaws.

It was summer vacation, and Martha was off from school. She was loving her new job as a full-time teacher. It gave her a great sense of accomplishment and fulfillment, unlike substituting, where she spent a day at a time babysitting a class.

For the first time, Martha decided to take a day, go to the mall and pamper herself. She began with a spa treatment, a massage and a facial. She then shopped the department stores for a new wardrobe and a few pairs of shoes. And finally, she enjoyed a facial makeover at the fragrance department. She looked so beautiful that she purchased over $100 in cosmetics so she could achieve the same effect at home.

On her way back from her shopping spree, she passed the company's headquarters. Payne's car was parked out front. Feeling euphoric about the new outfit she was wearing and her new makeup, she decided this was the perfect time to confront him.

Martha still could not get past the idea that Payne had fired the key employees in the company. And without consulting her. Even though he had assured her he would not take any major steps without her knowledge. The check amount shocked her. It gave her pause, and made her reconsider the threats she made to him.

Walking up to the desk at the front entrance, she said to the receptionist, "Hi. I'd like to see Harold."

"Do you have an appointment?"

"An appointment? I own this place."

"So sorry, I don't know you. Can I have your name?"

"I'm Martha Billings. Please let him know I'm here."

The receptionist told Christie about the visitor and after a few minutes wait, she brought Martha into Payne's office.

Without looking up, Payne said, "Martha, I asked you not to come here without an appointment. I'm extremely busy."

"I don't care what you said. It's still my company. And I'm not leaving until we talk."

Payne looked up from the report he was reading, and was shocked to see how beautiful she looked. Her face was radiant, and he couldn't take his eyes off her shapely breasts protruding from the tight-knit top. His reaction did not go unnoticed by Martha, and it made her feel good. He invited her to sit down, and more cordially he asked, "Okay, what is it that you want to discuss?"

"I want to know when you're leaving. I simply can't have you here."

"I'll be gone in a year. I work 16 hours a day, including weekends. And my effort is paying off big time. So, I'm not giving up the income that is rewarding me for my success. And you shouldn't complain. You share that income, and we'll sell this place for millions. But now is not the time."

"But you have not once, ever consulted me on the major decisions that affect this company and the employees. And that troubles me."

"So, get over it. You don't run a business on emotion. You run it on management skills. I'm sorry I had to fire those employees, but they were killing your business. And now you are about to become wealthy, and you're punishing me for doing my job. I just don't understand you."

"What you don't understand is loyalty, you bastard. Those people were dedicated to this company, and worked many weeks without a paycheck to keep this place alive. And you discarded them. Now I want you to leave."

"I will leave on my terms, as the contract states and not before. So, stop badgering me and let me get back to work."

Frustrated, Martha stood up and walked out. Payne watched her leave, lecherously staring at her butt under the clinging skirt. And he thought, *Wow, she looks better than ever. I should have thrown her across the desk and fucked her right here. And she would have loved it. I know that's why she came in today dressed like that. And if I had done it, maybe I could have changed her mind about my termination. But it's too late. My plan is coming together, and she'll regret having rejected me.*

21

Lawyering Up

As Martha drove home, she recognized that Payne would not go quietly. She was experiencing conflicting emotions. Her makeover aroused him immediately and that made her gloat. But she didn't accomplish her goal to get his commitment to leave. It was time to hire an attorney.

She made an appointment to meet with a lawyer recommended by her school principal. She needed help on how to get Harold Payne out of her life.

When she got to the attorney's office, she was a little surprised by his age. She expected him to be closer in age to her boss. He wore a light gray, three-piece suit that, along with his bowtie had been out of style for many years. Still the look, including the outdated office, all worked to give her a sense of security, experience and a calm demeanor.

And despite appearing much older, he had a warm smile and twinkling eyes. He also exhibited none of the harsh intensity that shrouded Payne's persona. Martha felt very comfortable with him the moment he gently shook her hand. It was like trading in a bully for grandfather.

"It's so nice to meet you, Mrs. Billings. I'm Carleton Hanks. Please tell me how I can help you."

Martha quickly took him through everything that happened with Payne since her husband's untimely passing, carefully leaving out any reference to her intimate relationship. She ended with the unexpected $50,000 check she received and her threat to terminate him for firing the employees.

Hanks listened intently. "It doesn't sound like you need help. What's the problem?"

"I'm caught between my anger at him not discussing key decisions with me, and how well his management is working. I also told him that I was going to get a new lawyer, fire him and hire a new CEO who respects me. I brought a copy of the agreement we have."

Hanks quickly read through the four-page document and said, "It is pretty standard and all looks in order for this kind of service structure. It's performance-based which is a benefit to you. However, the reward for him is very expensive. If the profit surges, Mr. Payne will receive extremely generous bonuses. Is that what he led you to believe?"

"Well, I didn't think much about it. We've been losing money since the company was founded. So, if he can turn it around, then he should be rewarded. How much are we talking about?"

"Hypothetically, if the company bills $1 million in any given quarter that is profitable, Payne would earn a bonus of $200,000."

"A million dollars? We never reached that in a year, so I'm not worried about him making disproportionate bonuses. But let's get to the heart of the matter. I want to be able to terminate him. He's been making some important decisions without my knowledge."

"Maybe you should be less worried about his decisions and more worried about how his termination would affect the company's performance at this time. For you to receive a $50,000 bonus check, he must have taken the correct management steps, even if you weren't consulted."

"But, don't you see? He promised to consult me on important matters."

"Mrs. Billings, often in business, decisions must be made quickly. They can't wait for a committee meeting, so to speak."

"Mr. Hanks, I own the company. I feel useless with no control. I can't allow him to run roughshod over everyone."

"The agreement gives him total run of the company. That kind of authority is pretty standard. Do you know enough about the operation to weigh in on key decisions? Also, if you fire him without cause, it will be very expensive for you. And, if you replace him now, it will be extremely disruptive, particularly when the company is turning around."

"Well, yes. That has occurred to me and is giving me pause."

"Then, let's not make any rash decisions here. What I suggest we do is have me call him and see if I can renegotiate his deal with better terms, and also see about having you be more involved with the firm's high-level management oversight."

Martha digested all of the risks and rewards. "You are right. That sounds like a smart way to move forward.

"I'm afraid you're in a very precarious position. But it will be important to change the rules somehow. Otherwise, it is going to cost you plenty."

"I was thinking irrationally when I threatened him, as I was so angry. Yes, he saved the company, but it's still my company. I need to be consulted on any important decisions. So, please call him, work out a deal that treats me more respectfully. And let me know what he says."

22

The Compromise

Just as he predicted, the sales volume kept climbing, each month by a larger percentage. Payne kept putting the new accounts into the recently created division, rather than on the main company's set of books. Even with the split, the ledger of the original company showed large sales increases. The double size warehouse soon filled up and the inventory was turning over rapidly.

With cash accumulating in both accounts, Payne began submitting invoices for his expenses and his bonuses. His bonus for the first eligible quarter earned him $420,000. He had Christie pay it in three monthly installments. He had already been receiving his increased weekly fee of $2,000. So did Martha. He also sent her another $50,000. All were paid out of the firm's main account.

While he was on another business trip, Payne got a call from attorney Carleton Hanks who left a message to call him back on his return. Extending professional courtesy, Payne phoned Hanks soon after he got back.

Hanks enumerated Martha's concerns and requests and asked that their agreement be modified, rather than have him terminated. Although Payne was relieved to avoid any legal proceedings, he stood his ground.

"Mr. Hanks, we both signed a document that is fair. I kept the vendors from closing down the firm, and drew no salary. Now that it is profitable, I expect to be properly compensated. This is a short-term relationship. I'll be gone as soon as the firm is stable. But she wants to throw me under the bus."

"Mr. Payne, that was a kneejerk reaction when she saw the changes you made without her knowledge. I have talked her down from that. And I also pointed out the obvious success you are achieving. She is already regretting her impulsive decision."

"The company now has a rapidly growing amount of equity. With all that I have done in a short time, this hysterical, overly naive woman threatened to fire me. I need her to back off and stay out of the office."

"So, here's what I'm recommending. I will be your point of contact, so we won't ever have a repeat of that scene in your office. The one item that bothers me is the formula for your bonuses. It's exorbitant. I would like to renegotiate a more reasonable formula. I would also like to adjust the terms of the termination, in the unlikely event that she decides to hire someone else in your place."

Payne countered. "The agreement is extremely fair and it is not negotiable. I took this assignment when the company had no money to pay me. I deliberately backend loaded my payout so the company could survive until I could get it turned around."

"I understand that, but over time, your reward could be extraordinary."

"We're not talking about me earning a vast, ongoing windfall. In another six to nine months, I will resign, which is sooner than I prefer. Mrs. Billings can then sell the company and be set for life."

"Okay, Mr. Payne. I'll go along with you and hold you to your timetable, and I will monitor the company through the financial statements. And maybe your vision proves accurate," said Hanks.

Before ending the call, Hanks advised Payne that if he didn't adhere to the timeframe he outlined, Mrs. Billings had ordered him to terminate Payne and sell the company.

Payne now had a clear deadline to complete his caper and leave.

23

Disappearing Witness

Sitting at his desk one morning, Payne was reviewing the financial report he was about to send to Carleton Hanks. Reminding himself of his conversation with Hanks confirmed that his clandestine plan was the right move. Martha did not want him to receive what he deserved. She'd rather sell than pay him what he rightfully earned.

Martha called. "Harold, I'm calling to make you understand how I feel since you came into my life."

"It's okay. We have a business deal. I'll soon be gone, and you'll get rewarded with a ton of money."

"It's not okay. And that's what you don't understand. It's not about the money. I care for the loyal people that worked for Ed, who sometimes went without a paycheck. And you went and fired them. That hurts me deeply."

"That's business. My job is to make the company successful so you have enough equity for the future."

"Not at the expense of those people you fired. You're a cold person. Look how you treated me. I was a sex object, not someone to indulge and love. You would come over, lay me and leave. You never even took your socks off, for God's sake."

"That's outrageous! I didn't treat you like a whore. I took you out to dinner. I gave you the sex you so desperately needed. Socks? Yeah. I hate to walk barefoot on your dirty floor."

"My floors are spotless. How dare you say that? And I wasn't desperate for sex. I was desperate for attention and intimacy. You just don't understand the difference."

"That's bullshit. You couldn't wait to get me in bed for a fuck. You needed a fast, hot orgasm, not intimacy. And I gave it to you."

"Oh, God. Why am I wasting my time with such an insensitive buffoon? Goodbye, Harold."

"Fuck you!" And to himself, "Who the fuck is she to tell me I'm insensitive? I'm easily the most caring guy in the world."

Following the call, Payne called Christie into his office and told her he was taking her out to lunch that day. She shot him a questioning look. He said, "We've got important business to discuss. Big changes are coming, and I want you prepared."

They went to a small restaurant and sat at a quiet table in the back. Christie was fidgeting and anxious to hear what was in his plans.

They ordered. Payne hesitated. "Christie, what are your long-term plans?"

"None, really. I'm trying to make as much money as I can. And with you paying me off the books plus the tip money from bartending, I've been able to save a lot."

"Do you have a boyfriend, a fiancé? Living with someone?"

"No. Why, you're not interested, are you? I mean, I like working for you, but no offense, you're not my type."

He smiled. "That's not why I'm asking. I am concerned about you, and with what's going to happen, I want you to be secure. Are you committed to living here in southern California?"

"I'm here by circumstance. If I had enough money and the right opportunity, I'd move, maybe to the mountains."

"Christie, this is exactly what I was hoping for. Going forward, I'll be asking you to make some changes to books.

"They will be questionable, but since I'm directing you, the liability is on me. For example, I want you to repost all the bonus checks to me as Accounts Payable/Product Inventory."

73

Christie looked at the ceiling, and asked, "Are these the big changes you mentioned?"

"There's more. It would be in your best interest to move in the next few months. You don't want to be here when questions are raised about the books.

"So, if you do as I instruct, I will give you a $150,000 bonus to help you get a fresh start somewhere else."

She was apprehensive, but also excited about the opportunity to leave the area that held so many bad memories. "Is this why you had me set up the second division?"

"Exactly. When I took over this company, it was virtually bankrupt, and Martha Billings would have lost her house because of it."

"What you did was nearly impossible. But she doesn't get it."

"I turned everything around for her. As you know, she's now getting big income from the company. And you saw how she treats me? She wants to fire me, the ungrateful bitch. I work 16 hours a day, and she is looking for a new CEO to replace me."

Christie sat there absorbing the details and feeling Payne's outrage. But something was missing. Her anger was too intense. Had he been sleeping with her?

"Well, I'm going to take what I earned, and leave her what's left. It won't be much, but it's more than she had when I started. Then she can let her new CEO rebuild the firm again."

"Harold, I see how hard you work. And I will always remember what you did for me. You had faith in me and I'm truly grateful."

"Thanks. "Think about where you want to move in three to six months. I'll coach you along the way and tell you what we need to do.

"And by the way, get all the locks at the office changed. By tomorrow."

24

Over the Edge

A couple of weeks later, at 5:30 one evening, Martha walked into the building. Christie had just left, and Payne was alone in his office. This time she wore more conservative clothing, and less makeup. Hiding his surprise as she walked in, he said, "What are you doing here? I told you not to barge into the office without an appointment."

"Be quiet, Harold, and listen to me. I can't get past how terribly you treated me when I last called you. I can't let it go. It made me realize how cruel and evil you are. I've decided that you must leave this company now."

"We have a contract. I'll leave in a few months, and you can do what you want with this place. But it'll be on my timetable."

"I can't stand to have you here. Reminding me I opened my heart to you is too painful. I hate you sitting at Ed's desk, making money from his company."

She stopped for a moment, pushing back the sobs that were forming in the back of her throat. She recovered. "If you don't leave immediately, I will get a court order to have you removed. I'm interviewing candidates to replace you, so my company will be just fine."

Resisting the urge to run out the door, Martha stood her ground as she blinked back the tears.

Seeing her discomfort, Payne gloated, thinking that she was getting what she deserved. In an angry tone, he said, "Tell you what. Have your lawyer call me. I'll discuss a timeframe with him that suits *my* needs. Now get the fuck out of here, I'm busy. And don't come back until I'm gone."

It took all her strength, but she refused to be intimidated. She inhaled deeply. "Don't you dare talk to me that way. I'll come in here anytime it suits me. How could I have had feelings for someone as heartless and callous as you? You are a seriously sick person."

Martha rushed out as her anger gave way to a flood of tears. Payne paced in the small office to quell his anger.

He shouted to the closed front entrance, "Fuck you, you ungrateful bitch! You still don't get what I did for you. You weren't even a good lay. And I've got the experience to know!"

Their exchange pushed him to move up his timing. Now he was going all out and take her fucking company down.

25

Finalizing the Details

The next day, following Martha's intrusion, Payne called Diego Santos and told him he had to move up the exit date. The Brazilian said everything was set. All Payne had to do was give him the exact day. Done deal.

Christie updated Payne on her plans. She would move to Colorado. "I chose Vail, a ski resort town that catered to the wealthy ski and party crowd. I'll be handling the books for a bar and restaurant group, and managing one of the restaurants."

"That sounds perfect."

"The owner is going to call you for a reference."

"I will give him the most glowing testimonial he's ever heard. Now, here's what you do. Work through next week and then resign."

He told her he would give her enough money to buy a late model SUV, make the trip to Vail, rent a nice condo, and have plenty left over for unexpected costs. Plus, a little nest egg for the future.

He gave her detailed instructions. "Pay cash for everything, close your bank and credit card accounts. Take only what you can fit in the SUV, and give away everything else.

"When you get to Vail, don't open a bank account or take out a credit card for a few months. After that, you're clear. It will be me they'll chase, and trust me, they will never find me."

Christie was surprised and frightened by how dangerous Payne's plan was. It made her want to get away quickly.

Comforted by how her life was about to change, she tried to push the fear out of her mind.

Payne leaned back in his chair and put his feet on the desk, delighting over his embezzlement plan. After Martha's relentless attacks on him, it was over. He was getting his reward, taking everything, and leaving her where she was before he showed up.

26

Loose Ends

Over the next couple of weeks, Payne sent checks from the company's secondary bank to a numbered account at a bank in the Cayman Islands. And those funds were later transferred to a bank in São Paolo, Brazil. He followed Diego Santos' instructions exactly. As he was draining the account, he gradually cashed a series of checks totaling $150,000. He then closed the account.

At the end of the month, Payne called the remaining four employees into his office and told them starting Monday the entire facility would be closed for two weeks for fumigation and some alterations. They'd get the time off with pay.

The staff was delighted with the paid time off. They had been putting in extensive hours and needed the break. The receptionist sat there wondering what she would do with her time, other than sleep late in the morning.

Payne called Christie and asked her to stop by the office after hours one day. He handed her a briefcase with the $150,000. He also asked where she kept the records of the secondary account, and the backup disks for all the computers. After she left, he shredded all the files, including the main account, and took the disks. He also removed the computer hard drives and took them.

Before leaving the building that night, Payne put all the shredded waste into the recycle bins on the loading platform. He then drove downtown to a large strip mall that housed a pizza parlor, an upscale restaurant, and a coffee shop. He drove around the back and tossed the smashed disks and the hard drives into the dumpsters.

The next morning, he met with his law office secretary. He told her that he was closing the practice. He had her write a letter to the landlord advising that they were leaving. He had her write herself a check for two months' salary as severance. She should also hire someone to take all the files and move them to a storage facility. Leaving the law office for the last time, Payne closed the bank account, taking the remaining funds in cash.

With that complete, Payne stopped by his shabby studio apartment, packed his suitcase, and went to the office. He was an hour early for the pickup, but that didn't keep him from pacing constantly in a fruitless attempt to control his anxiety.

27

A New Beginning
November, 1993, São Paulo, Brazil

Gerard Morbus sipped single malt scotch as he surveyed the sights from his balcony in a luxury high rise building. The beautifully appointed unit was on a wide boulevard in a wealthy neighborhood of opulent homes, multifamily apartments and exclusive hotels. The ornate, gilded furniture and expensive decorative accessories reflected the affluence of the area.

São Paulo is a city of 12 million, shared by multicultural people of extreme wealth and a large population of desperately poor residents living in high-crime areas. The rich are constant victims of kidnapping, theft, and other crimes, so that awareness of surroundings was critical to survival at all times.

Brazilians dine at 9 or later, so the energy level picks up at night, attracting strollers and street peddlers. But often, one block off the main thoroughfares can be dangerous and sometimes fatal.

It was approaching sunset, and the city was glowing. He expected Salete Pereira to arrive at any moment to give him his daily lesson in Portuguese and tell him more about his new home city, São Paulo.

He looked forward to her visits, as she was the only person in this vast, sprawling city that he knew. But it was more than that. At five-foot two, Salete was petite with a very lovely face that sparkled when she smiled. She had a lithe body with perfect curves and beautifully sculpted legs like so many Brazilian women. Her height and smooth skin made her look much younger than her 40 years. And in keeping with the other well-dressed women here, her stylish, expensive clothes heightened her sensual shape.

Salete was gifted with twinkling brown eyes and dark curly hair. She spoke fair English with a slight accent and was both well-educated and street smart. She also had an inner strength you could sense. It made you realize that this was a woman who made her own decisions. And yet, she was the kind of person you wanted to be near.

When she arrived, Gerard offered her a drink, but she said, "Let's take a walk and have strolling lesson tonight. I want to show you more of the city, and we can later stop for a drink."

They wandered around the neighborhood streets, with elaborate glass and polished aluminum and steel residential buildings, and attractive retail boutiques and shops below. She pointed out signs and translated the words, each time asking him to repeat them. During this walking tour, Salete explained that there were retail streets devoted to designated types of merchandise. She showed him streets where all the shops carried women's clothing. Some sold only shoes, jewelry, or other goods. He was fascinated.

After about an hour, they stopped at a hotel bar and ordered glasses of wine. The lounge was nearly empty, except for a couple of businessmen at the bar. They moved to a small table, and Gerard asked her about her childhood and where she grew up. She repeated his question in Portuguese and made him ask her again in that language.

He stumbled through it, forgetting a couple words and mispronouncing others. This made her giggle, and smiling, she responded, "Is not interesting. I grew up very poor in other part of city."

"That's okay. I want to learn all I can about you."

"Diego told me. When I was little, my parents had eight children and no money. My father gave me and my brother Diego to a couple who could not have children."

"That must have been traumatic for you."

"I have no memory. When I was eleven, my new parents were killed by robbers, and we were left to be orphans. We stayed in apartment for a while, but when Children's Court found us, they put us in orphanage. Conditions there were very terrible. There was little food, and they beat us a lot."

"That sounds horrible. How did you survive?"

"One night, Diego took me and we escaped. We lived in the streets until he could find a little tin shanty for us to stay. The church gave us food and made me go to class. I worked after school for rich family to take care of their children and to do chores around the house. The wife liked me and gave me food and extra money."

"You were fortunate to have someone help you like that."

"Yes, but one day, when we were alone, the husband had his way with me, and I ran away from that house. When Diego found out, he beat husband very bad, and then told the wife."

"My God, the guy is lucky Diego didn't kill him."

"Diego always took care of me and kept me going to school. That was best because I learn English and math."

"It's hard to imagine growing up like that. How did you become successful?"

"I had many jobs. I worked in office. I worked in restaurants. The money was good, but the men always tried to take advantage of me.

"Later, I decorate and buy furniture for people that come here from other countries. Everything in your apartment I do. I selected and bought.

"Diego gets me work from his clients, like with you. He is a lot of time in US and some other countries, but he still watches out for me."

"Well, you have excellent taste. I love the way you did my place."

Gerard suggested dinner. "Is there a love interest in your life?"

Giggling, she answered, "Love interest? You mean like boyfriend? No, I don't go much on dates. And it would be difficult to have a boyfriend that Diego would consent."

"Well then, there's no chance for me. Diego would never approve of me."

"Why not? You are not like his other clients. Most of them are criminals and in drugs. You are gentleman with education, wear nice clothes. And you don't look at me like the men with lust and hunger in their eyes."

"Thank you. I respect you and I respect Diego. I would never do anything to offend either of you."

After dinner, he offered to accompany her home, but she laughed and said, "Oh, no. It is much too dangerous for you than for me. No one will dare touch me. I will walk with you and then take taxi to my home."

28

The First Date

Salete continued to tutor Gerard for the next month. He was learning the language, at least enough to communicate with the locals. Of key importance was where to travel within the city and what times to avoid certain areas, especially after dark. He was getting to know the mores and customs. But his knowledge only extended to the immediate neighborhood.

One morning, they were having cappuccino at a neighborhood café. Gerard was noticeably nervous and out of character for his self-assured persona. Stumbling over his words, he surprised Salete. He blurted out, "I want, I want to ask you out. I mean on a date. Would you accept? And must I get Diego's permission? Will he be upset?"

Salete was laughing at his clumsy request. This vocal American with his smooth, dominant presence could not invite her on a date without completely losing his nerve.

She reached across the table and touched the back of his hand. "I would like that, and I am sure my brother would approve. So, what will we do that we are not doing together almost every day?"

"Salete, it's work. You are teaching and I am learning. I want to have a romantic evening with you. Let's get dressed up and go to the finest restaurant in the city for a wonderful dinner. You pick."

She raised a perfect eyebrow, "And after dinner?"

"There are no plans and no expectations beyond dinner."

Squeezing his hand, and with a big smile, she said, "Geraldo, you are truly a gentleman, and I look forward to our date."

The following evening, Salete came to Gerard's place to pick him up. She wore a scarlet silk sheath with a short skirt that accented her Brazilian hips and tanned legs. He opened the door, suddenly breathless at the sight of her. She smiled. "Olá Geraldo, I look okay? I have a taxi waiting downstairs."

He was wearing a thousand-dollar tan suit, and a white shirt with a Jerry Garcia tie. As they walked to the elevator, he couldn't take his eyes off her firm butt and shapely legs in her red high heels.

The cab dropped them off in front of Figueira Rubaiyat, no doubt one of the most famous and expensive restaurants in the city. Salete had reserved a table in the center of the restaurant, under the giant fig tree over 100 years old. The landmark tree extends through the glass-paneled roof and towers 165 feet above the dining room. Gerard was in awe of this magnificent setting that Salete chose for the special first date. She stood there smiling as he walked around this fifty-foot-wide tree that completely dominated the restaurant.

For the next three hours they sipped wine, ate six courses of Brazilian food, and finished the evening with glasses of fine port.

When the taxi returned to Gerard's apartment, he asked, "Will you come up and stay for a while?"

She smiled, and gave him a brief but very passionate kiss, pressing her body to him. That move not only aroused him from his toes to his ears but encouraged his expectations, as well.

Dashing his hopes, she put her hands on his chest. "No. We cannot do that now. Once I sleep with you, there is no turning back. I not want a relationship with easy sex. I insist only on a total commitment, so you must think hard about that, and when you are ready, and you are sure you want to be with me only, to love, then we will do this. I would like to be with you, Geraldo. And so, you must decide when you can be ready to do this."

She slipped in the cab and went home. Gerard stood there, watching the taxi disappear around a corner. His synapses were exploding in his brain, still anticipating the euphoric sex encounter that would not happen. He desperately wanted her sexually, and he held her in high esteem, but was he ready to make a lifetime commitment? He honestly didn't have the answer to that question. And if he hurt her in any way, he was certain The Brazilian would leave his broken, mutilated body in an alley somewhere in a *favela*.

Gerard was still haunted by a brief, two-year marriage in his early twenties. She was a wonderful, warm person that anyone could love. She had so much to give, but he was flawed. He had known in his heart that he was incapable of sharing the love necessary to sustain any kind of conjugal relationship. And he couldn't be sure he could do it now.

It started with his loveless childhood in an alcohol-fueled home. And then in his self-centered, ruthless career, he had become colder and more impersonal through the years. He had no choice but to simply maintain their relationship for now and see how it progressed.

Gerard truly cared for Salete. Could she be the force to make that change?

29

Impulsive Decision

Gerard's educational relationship with Salete continued for several months, as he grew more comfortable in his adopted city. The time had arrived when she was no longer needed regularly. She mentioned that to him one evening when they walked through a market. He panicked.

He had become her constant companion. And he had grown fond of her, far beyond the sexual attraction. He also recognized just how horny he was. He had not had sex in over two years.

Salete said she had an offer to work with a family in Rio on the coast for three months and was considering it.

The response that Gerard blurted out was so unlike him he questioned himself. "Salete, you can't leave me now. I need you." He had never depended on anyone in his life. How could he have articulated this weakness? But he meant it. And he didn't regret it.

Having spent so much time with him, and being well aware of his hard edge and bluster that occasionally emerged, Salete was as shocked by his reaction as he was. She took his hand as they walked and looked up to him saying, "My rules are the same. I will only stay if you make sincere commitment. But I know how you feel and I doubt you can very much change."

Stopping and turning to her, he took both her hands and stated, "I'm a different person. Brazil is changing me. You are changing me. I can feel it. It's all having an effect on me and I want to be with you day and night. Will you take a chance on this damaged individual that is trying to heal?"

Salete could see how he grew more relaxed and calmer, and she was encouraged by this change. His sincerity and honesty got to her. "Yes, Geraldo. I think maybe you are now ready."

"Then let's live together immediately!"

"I will spend nights with you, but for now, I keep my apartment also. Tonight, let's have a light dinner, and tomorrow I bring breakfast, and some clothes to stay. And I tell the family in Rio, no. I cannot work for them."

Later that night, back home after dinner, Gerard reflected on their conversation. He realized that he panicked when she told him about her new assignment. He knew he was lost without her. But the question was still there. *Could he be a good husband and make her happy?* He concluded being pushed into this unplanned commitment would force him to become the person he needed to be, and the person she would want him to be.

30

The Adjustment Period

The next morning, Salete arrived with a suitcase and a shopping bag full of pastries and other breakfast foods. She dropped her luggage in the bedroom, and arranged the food on platters. Gerard had already made coffee, so they sat and ate breakfast.

It was a comical scene as they each wore a broad smile and barely spoke. They were suddenly uncomfortable, with both of them having difficulty making small talk. So, they stared at each other and enjoyed the food and the idea that they were about to share their lives. Recognizing what was happening, they suddenly burst out laughing at each other's discomfort.

She cleaned the table, and washed the dishes. Gerard went into the bedroom and cleaned out a closet and a dresser for her clothes. As Salete unpacked, he straightened out the entire flat. He moved some chairs around, so they could sit closer together.

She checked out the partially filled pantry and refrigerator, making a grocery list and they walked to the market. Both of them acted like kids, as they explored the stores and the stalls, finding ingredients to make *Feijoada* and other local dishes.

Gerard let her lead the way, as it was apparent that she had very specific ideas about what she wanted to buy and which items she purchased, particularly the meats and produce. They also stopped at a wine shop to stock up on several varieties of wine. Salete selected a bottle of *cachaça*, the native liquor to make the Brazilian cocktail, *caipirinha*.

Laden with shopping bags, they took a taxi back to the apartment.

Salete announced, "To celebrate our living with each other, I make wonderful dinner for you tonight. It will be Brazilian beef dish, slowly cooked you will love."

"That's sounds exciting. Let me help you."

She spread out the ingredients on the counter and told Gerard to peel the cucumbers and clean the mushrooms. He struggled with both. She giggled watching his awful effort as she was cutting the beef. Finally, she said, "Leave the kitchen. I will prepare the dinner. You will later clean up mess."

As the dinner was slow cooking in a large pot, he opened a bottle of wine and they sat on the balcony. And even from the small terrace, they could smell tomato, onions, manioc, cilantro and okra simmering with the beef. Salete set the table and lit candles.

She wanted their first dinner together at home to be very cozy and romantic. They savored each course and finished the wine. Gerard brought out a bottle of rare cognac and two snifters. They each slowly sipped two glasses with the anticipation of newlyweds. Then he took her hand and led her into the bedroom. He gently undressed her down to her bra and thong, which were both skimpy and erotic.

As she helped him out of his clothes, he could barely contain himself. He took off her undergarments and lightly pushed her onto the bed without removing the expensive bedspread. With very little foreplay, he climbed on her and in her, reaching an orgasm in minutes, long before she was fully aroused. As he rolled over to catch his breath, Salete laid there unfulfilled and disappointed.

After a minute or two, she said to him, "Geraldo, get up before we ruin duvet."

They both got up and removed the cover, and he went into the bathroom to clean up. Salete climbed back into bed under the bedsheets. Gerard got in next to her, still without saying a word. Turning to him she chided with anger in her voice, "Geraldo, that was most terrible. You no make love. You make sex like clumsy, lustful gringo."

Shocked, he responded, "But Salete, you are even more beautiful naked. You had me so excited I had no control. I came almost immediately."

"What about me? I have to feel it too. You not know, a woman gets aroused more slowly? I have to teach you to make love, not have sex. And your underpants. I wear beautiful lace to make you excited. And you wear white shorts to make me laugh. And why you wear socks?"

She'd make it her mission to teach this gauche American to become a fulfilling love partner.

31

Reckless Endangerment

Following their dreadful first sexual encounter, Salete patiently taught him how to satisfy her. And while he got better at it, his attention span was too short to spend hours lying in bed kissing, talking and fondling in between bouts of intercourse. And while their sex life was less than blissful, it was a marked improvement from the disastrous beginning. Fortunately, everything else in the relationship was satisfying and enjoyable.

After a month of living together, Gerard went out to buy an engagement ring to surprise her. As an obvious American in São Paulo, he didn't stand a chance of getting a good deal without her by his side. Remembering that Salete told him about the streets that all carried the same merchandise, he wandered through the open-air markets and neighborhoods, searching for the jewelry market. He wanted a store that carried high quality, exclusive gemstones.

After rejecting a few stalls and stores, a local man walked up to him, and in broken English asked if he would like to buy a *special* ring. The young Portuguese man then said, "Follow me for very good price."

Without thinking, Gerard let the man lead him through a series of alleys, and in minutes, they were at the end of a deserted courtyard. Abruptly, two men emerged from a door and the three of them slowly surrounded Gerard. The first man snarled, "Senor, no trouble. Give your money and your watch."

Gerard backed against a wall and prepared to defend himself. He was not about to give up his Rolex and the cash he had with him to buy the ring. The men were inches shorter than him and looked like they hadn't eaten in several days. Although he was scared, he felt certain he could chase them off. With his adrenaline surging, he picked up a stick laying on the ground, stepped forward and began swinging it in their direction. "Come on, you fucking punks. You want my money? Try to take it. I'll beat the living shit out of all of you!"

When each of the men took out a knife, Gerard realized he had underestimated his predicament and that the situation was dire. Now, he was petrified, and shouted for help. He flailed at them with the stick, which now seemed like a puny weapon against three knives, but as they closed in on him, his stick landed several painful strikes to their heads, arms and shoulders. It only made them even angrier.

Gerard kept turning in a tighter circle as the men moved closer. And in a flash, one of them kicked the back of his wrist and the stick flew out of his hand. With his bravado and paltry weapon gone, and the knives flicking at his face, he knew he was doomed. The leader snarled, "Now you die, stupid gringo."

But suddenly, a woman behind him yelled, *"Pare! Fique longe dele."* Stop! Get away from him.

After warning them to halt, she then said that he was a friend of Diego Santos. If they wanted to live, they would let him go, unharmed.

Hearing Diego's name, the men turned and ran out of the courtyard. Gerard turned and was shocked to see a furious Salete standing there. "Geraldo, how could you be stupid like this? Everything I teach you about this city, wasted. You would die today."

Sheepishly, he responded, "I was trying to buy you a special gift."

"Geraldo, you only shop in the places I bring you. Never go to *favelas* that are not safe. Is far too dangerous. If a friend did not see you leave shopping area and call me, I could not rescue you."

The incident left Gerard badly shaken. He never thought about how treacherous São Paulo could be, even areas just steps from active, affluent shopping districts. It would be days before he would even step out of the apartment. Did he make the right choice of settling in this beautiful but very dangerous city?

32

The Wedding

A few weeks later, when Salete was away at an all-day business event, Gerard dared to venture out to buy that special ring. This time he walked to the shops on the boulevards in the nearby upscale section of the city. Fortunately, he found exactly what he was looking for. But as expected, he woefully paid over $3,000 more than the exquisite diamond ring was worth.

That night, he took her out to dinner and before their first glass of wine, he made his proposal, "Salete, you bring me so much happiness. I want to be with you for life. Do you feel like I do and want to be together?" He took out the ring and showed it to her.

She hadn't expected it, as she was certain that he would discuss it with her, first. And then he would have her bring him to a jewelry shop where she could negotiate the purchase.

Still, she was ecstatic. "Geraldo, what a beautiful ring and great surprise. You make me feel happy. And for me I see you changing also."

The next day, Salete called her brother and told him the news. Diego was not thrilled. He knew too much about Gerard, and worried about how he would treat his sister.

He flew down before the wedding to confront Gerard and make sure he understood the consequences, should he fail to make Salete blissfully happy. He also wanted to warn him that, as the future spouse of his sister, his days of questionable or illegal ethics and business practices were over.

Salete made plans for their simple wedding and a honeymoon to an exotic location. She wanted to have a church ceremony, followed by a quiet dinner party at a fine restaurant.

Diego arrived a few days later and over lunch engaged Gerard in his *Come to Jesus* meeting. Gerard had both fear and respect for Diego, so he took his advice and his veiled threats seriously.

He had no plans to return to the business world, as he had enough money to live out his life in opulent comfort in Brazil. He was also confident he could maintain the relationship he had with Salete and keep her happy. He told Diego that it was her caring, selfless personality that had so totally changed his attitude and his character. And so, their wedding plans moved forward.

At Salete's insistence, they chose a small church near where she grew up on the outskirts of the city. She wore a white dress and tiny veil that beautifully contrasted her hair and complexion. And even in this modest attire, she looked sexy and exotic. Diego, in a dark suit, similar to Gerard's, served both as the best man and the person presenting the bride. His girlfriend, who Salete knew from childhood, was maid of honor.

Following the brief service, a rented limousine took them to a small restaurant in Cantareira, where the owner was a friend of Diego. The location offered a magnificent view of the mountains overlooking São Paulo.

Because of their lengthy relationship, the chef owner prepared a feast that outdid any fine dining experience in all of this famous region. It consisted of multiple courses, each paired with a wine that complemented the exotic flavors of the dish.

The entrees included the restaurant's version of *Moqueca*, a stew made with pieces of fish and shrimp cooked in coconut milk. The beef dish featured an unusual combination of rare spices. Among the desserts served was *Mousse de Maracuja*, a pudding made with passion fruit.

Every platter delivered a different taste sensation, and was garnished like a work of art.

When the celebration finally ended, the limo took the newlyweds back to their apartment and then drove Diego and his lover to the small flat he kept in the city.

The next day, Salete and Gerard flew to Lima, Peru for a vacation exploring the exotic destinations in that country.

She had booked a private tour lasting three weeks and was very excited about their first visit to this country. It started with the sights and dining experiences in the country's largest city, Lima. The mountain destinations, in particular, offered an exhilarating adventure for them both. They particularly enjoyed exploring the ancient ruins, including Intihuatana and Machu Picchu.

After a few days of hiking the ruins, Salete showed no signs of fatigue, but Gerard's soft body was rebelling. They cut the tour short and returned to São Paulo.

33

Gastronomic Indulgences

Home from their exhaustive vacation, they settled into a routine lifestyle. Gerard insisted that Salete give up the personal service assignments that she got from Diego. He did not want her to take any work from single men, where the possibility of compromising situations and the potential of danger existed for her. He encouraged her interior decorating and personal shopping projects, which she loved and kept her active.

Gerard grew bored with his lifestyle, and he read profusely. He even attempted to write a book. He soon realized it required perseverance and discipline, plus constant review and rewriting, none of which were his strong points.

In his writing, he failed to recognize that the protagonist was based on himself. And the character had all the superior qualities and virtues that he thought he possessed. Upon reading his loosely composed, partially completed manuscript, he realized it was a dull, plotless story that merely venerated him, and rambled with no end in sight. So, he gave up his writing career before it began.

The one activity they both looked forward to was having dinner at the endless selection of restaurants, both local cafes and fine dining establishments. Gerard particularly liked discovering new places to experience the varied cuisine that was offered by the vast number of restaurants in this bustling city.

They dined at the long-established *Fuentes*, famous for its Paella, as well as a small neighborhood dining gem called

Tabapua that truly mastered the art of lamb preparation. They found restaurants that served traditional food from the Amazon region, Africa, Syria, French bistros, and more.

This dining pleasure from both the frequency and consumption of so many multi-course meals was beginning to reflect on Gerard's weight. He was now 20 pounds heavier than when he arrived in São Paulo. The much more disciplined Salete easily maintained her gorgeous shape and year-round tan.

Their sex life, while much improved from its disastrous beginning, was still not up to Salete's desires. She continued to work on Gerard's performance but recognized that it would not be what she had dreamed about. He was too self-centered to put her desires first and satisfy her needs.

34

Escape from Boredom

Over the next several years, Gerard's plodding, single-dimensional lifestyle caused him to become depressed, as there wasn't anything to stimulate his mind. Salete, on the other hand, focused on her ever-growing decorating and personal shopping business.

At one point, she rented a small warehouse to store the art, accessories and furniture that she discovered on her shopping tours. She called herself *A Senhora do Saco*, The Bag Lady. While she deposited an escalating amount of money into their joint checking account, it was dwindling. This had far more to do with Brazil's growing inflation rate than their lavish spending. And it was depleting their financial holdings.

Right from the beginning, when Gerard moved to São Paulo, he had Salete handling his bill paying and finances. He considered bookkeeping to be women's work. He was therefore not aware that his balances were dropping, and it was Salete's income that kept them in their luxurious lifestyle. And since Gerard was so oblivious of the money outflow, she was certain that he had other funds stashed somewhere that she didn't know about.

In the meantime, Gerard was going stir-crazy but had no interest in participating in Salete's business. He planned a vacation to try deep-sea fishing. His research led him to a small resort in the heart of the sports fishing region of Costa Rica on the Pacific Ocean.

He made a phone call to the resort. The owner said his resort itself was fully booked for the next two months, but he had a small mansion a half-mile into town that Gerard could use. It was more expensive than the resort rooms, but very private, and included all the resort amenities.

Gerard booked it for one week, saying, "This sounds like it exactly fits my needs. I am looking for a quiet destination without a flood of tourists. And I want to try some deep-sea fishing."

"Have you caught sailfish in the Pacific before? It's not an experience for the timid."

"I've lived in California, and I've done it all."

35

Releasing Bodily Fluids

When Gerard checked in at the resort, he asked the owner, Carlos to recommend and book him on a small charter fishing boat. He was excited about the challenge of going out into the Pacific to try his hand at offshore fishing.

The mansion turned out to be perfect. It was an older Key West style building updated and maintained in excellent condition. There were two other renters, both men, but he was the sole guest in the eastern wing with its own entrance. The interior of the house, with its teak and ebony paneled library, was fully stocked with complimentary wine and liquor. It was all appointed for a man's taste.

At 6 am Gerard boarded the 36-foot fishing boat. The captain and mate greeted him in broken English. Both men had the weather-beaten faces and dark skin that resulted from years on the water. The boat, although seaworthy, was in the final stages of useful life.

As they left the harbor, Gerard was fascinated by the turquoise water, and for a while he leaned over looking for fish. Once on the open water, the hour and a half ride out to the canyons seemed like it took days. The mate looked at the captain and they both laughed, knowing that their novice passenger was going to get seasick.

Long before they got to the best fishing area, Gerard delivered a steady chum that included his breakfast and the previous night's expensive dinner over the side. Finally, when there was nothing left in his digestive system, his stomach calmed and he was ready to try fishing.

Given his ADHD personality, fishing was not the ideal sport for him. His short attention span was not suited for sitting in a chair patiently waiting for some phantom fish to attach itself to his line. And his fair skin, even with a heavy layer of sunscreen, did not react well to the blistering sun. He quickly gave up on deep-sea fishing.

Gerard had the mate take a picture of him in the sports fishing chair, fighting a non-existent trophy-sized sailfish. He couldn't wait to return to land.

The next evening, after his stomach found its way back into his abdomen and reconnected itself to his intestines, he ate nearby. Inquiring about the nightlife in the area, his waiter suggested he visit the bar directly across the street from the mansion. He described the bar as the destination for *enjoying the local hospitality*. Gerard stopped for a drink on the way back.

The place was not what he expected. The lights were dim and the music was soft and romantic. It had a large circular bar where several men nursed their drinks. And walking around the perimeter was a parade of attractive women, prostitutes dressed in provocative outfits.

Gerard ordered a single malt scotch on the rocks. Before long a tall, Hispanic woman came over and sat next to him. She was maybe five-feet, eight with protruding nipples pressing against her blouse. She asked if he would like company while he enjoyed his drink. Her English was good, although heavily accented. She told him her name was Anna and asked how he was enjoying his vacation.

They made small talk, and then she asked if he would like to take her to his place for the night. He answered, "I have to be up early in the morning, but if you'd like to come over for a drink and stay awhile, that I would like."

A few minutes later, they were back at the mansion and he took her up to his room. When the door closed, she said, "Would you like to have sex with me?"

And he answered, "Why don't you take your clothes off and give me a blow job."

"You like mouth sex? I will make your head explode."

As she undressed, he slid off his shoes and put his pants, neatly folded, on the chair. He sat on the edge of the bed while she stripped down directly in front of him. Her breasts were inches from his face. They were small and firm, with large protruding nipples. He roughly fondled them and put one breast in his mouth. She nuzzled him back on the bed and began running her hands over his testicles and his penis, which was quickly hardening. Putting some K-Y jelly on her hands, she continued to massage his scrotum as she licked the tip of his penis.

With all the activity around his crotch, Gerard was not sure exactly what she was doing but he was aroused in a way like he had never experienced. With her mouth around his penis and her tongue licking the tip, she started pushing a strand of large beads into his anus. This only brought him to the edge of climax. At that point, she ran his rock-hard penis in and out of her mouth and then began pulling the beads out of his ass. He ejaculated like a geyser, rocking his butt up and down on the bed. As he recovered, she laughed and remarked, "See, I told you I make your head explode, but you thought it would be one on your shoulders."

For the next five nights, Gerard went to dinner, and then walked to the bar for his scotch. Each evening, he met another beautiful woman who wanted to come back to his room for a sexual interlude. He never tried fishing again and spent his days in the library reading books and anticipating his next nightly adventure.

36

Thieves in the Night

When he returned home, Gerard was rested, relaxed, and sexually spent. Salete had prepared a delicious Brazilian meal for his return, in expectation of a celebratory evening. She missed him as her desires peaked.

He was delighted to be home with her, yet he was burned out from the variety of sexual partners in Costa Rica. He was not in the mood for sex, particularly missionary style, which Salete preferred. She had been expecting him to be there for her, so he faked his desire and enthusiasm.

Lying in bed after his usual rush to clean up after their encounter, he told her how much he enjoyed the calm serenity of his stay at the mansion. The excitement of the fishing had been so therapeutic that he had decided he would return once every three or four months to recharge his batteries.

After the first few days of catching up, their relationship quickly fell back into its dull routine. And Salete kept busy with her thriving business venture.

About a year later, tragedy struck the business. There was a break-in at the warehouse late one night. A security guard who patrolled her building was shot and killed. Salete was devastated. After years of effort to accumulate this vast inventory of high-end furniture, accessories and decorative accouterments, they were all gone. And this security officer had lost his life.

She told Gerard, "The police will do nothing. They were surely bribed to stay away from the scene while that gang of thieves could take time to put everything from the warehouse in their vans before they left. I am having to call Diego. He will get back all my furniture and punish these cowards."

"Salete, calm down. You can't call Diego whenever you are in trouble. More people will get hurt. What if there's retribution?"

"But these *bastardos* stole what took years to collect. We have to get it back."

"Forget the furniture. Forget the business. With more crime every day, it is getting to be too dangerous to live here. You made lots of money and insurance will cover the losses."

"The insurance not pay for my time to find this beautiful furniture."

"We should move back to the states where it is safer. I will find a city where we can live, and you can start up a new decorator service. The insurance money from the loss will help you get started."

Salete agreed with him, and she also thought if Gerard was back in the US, their married life would show an improvement. She was convinced that if he had some kind of outside interest to keep him busy, he would be more interested and attentive at night in bed.

Within a month, the claim was paid. Gerard was surprised it was nearly $2 million. It went a long way to replenishing their funds that had been depleted by their luxury lifestyle without any income from him.

37

Finding Paradise
November 2010, Sarasota, FL

Gerard had researched various regions of the US to find the ideal location. He wanted to be in a small city where there would be little or no chance of someone uncovering his past. He selected Sarasota, Florida. It was a resort city on the Gulf with an affluent population of about 70,000. And it was rich in art and culture which would benefit Salete's business model. They purchased a home on a large lot in a secluded part of the suburbs away from the downtown area.

Arriving in the city, they explored the world-famous Siesta Key Beach with its white quartz sand, stretching the length of a football field between the dunes and the water's edge. They traveled downtown along the bayfront, packed with sailboats and motor yachts, drove by all the art galleries on Palm Avenue, and past the opera house, theaters and performing arts center, enthralled by it all. Gerard commented, "This is truly Paradise."

Salete restarted her business, which began slowly as she had no referral base to help her grow. Gerard realized that his *retirement* account, which included Salete's insurance money, was dwindling. Even in Florida with its lower cost of living and no state income taxes, it would not last long enough given the lifestyle they had expected. Besides, he needed some stimulation, but the kind that could generate income. He could not risk trying to apply to practice law in Florida. That left business consulting as the best choice for him.

Gerard checked out the business community and networked. The Gulf Coast was hard hit by the real estate crash, and most companies connected to the development and construction were struggling. He sent out letters to small local firms he surmised direly needed his help. Although he secured a few clients, they were short-lived and did not generate the cash flow he sought.

He finally landed a client who had potential to generate serious income. It was an air conditioning company that was facing a strong base of bigger, well-established competition. Despite their large volume using discounted pricing, they were not profitable.

Through his efforts after about a year, the sales grew, and the revenue grew even faster. Dissatisfied with the fees he was receiving, Gerard requested an increase from the owner. Refusing his request, the owner explained, "I'm staying with the contract that you wrote. At the end of the year, we can renegotiate it."

Angered and disappointed, Gerard padded his expenses to squeeze a little more income from the firm. He took Salete out for an expensive dinner at Michael's On East and put the $200+ cost on his expense report as dinner with one of the company's large builder clients. The proprietor quickly uncovered Gerard's petty theft and confronted him, demanding he return the unearned monies.

Instead of complying, Gerard shouted, "Listen, you dumb motherfucker, you don't know a damn thing about running a business. If I walk out, this place will go down like lead balloon."

The proprietor was embarrassed by the exchange in front of the staff. "Yes, leave now. You're a low-level thief."

"Look at all the money I put in your pocket. But, did you think to give me a small bonus? Fuck no! Instead, you bitch about the paltry fee you pay me, and confront me over a few extra bucks that I took because I deserve it. So, go fuck yourself. Good luck holding this shithole excuse for a company together."

After his abrupt departure from the assignment, Gerard did not immediately seek another consulting client. He decided the small business owners in this community were small-minded, and were not willing to pay him what he was worth.

After a few years of inactivity, Gerard again took on small consulting assignments, but none of them were consequential or fulfilling. He was bored. Despite his lackluster results for generating income, it did not deter him from taking his periodic trips down to Costa Rica. He justified his need for these sojourns by convincing himself that they helped keep his mind sharp and inspired him to perform better.

38

Meeting the Savior
May 2015, Quepos, Costa Rica

Ronald Lawson arrived at La Concha Hotel & Resort a week after the shipment arrived. Carlos Diaz, the resort's owner, greeted him. Over coffee, Ronald explained, "I'll be going fishing tomorrow, and after that, I could work with the maintenance team to begin the installation."

Carlos expressed his excitement about having the new system put in. He pointed to Costa Rica's strong focus on the ecology and water conservation which was critically short in his Central American country.

After a few days of training and oversight during the installation, Ronald was relaxing at the tiki bar enjoying a cocktail. Carlos came over to him and invited him to dinner that night in the city. He was meeting with a frequent resort guest who was staying at the rental property that he owned downtown.

When he arrived at the mansion, Lawson was immediately impressed with the quality of the exotic wood species and the beautiful finishes. The sitting room had a wonderful Old World feel and fragrance. When they entered the foyer of the guesthouse, Carlos introduced him to Gerard Morbus. Being his affable self, Lawson reached out and shook his hand. Gerard seemed a little uncomfortable accepting the handshake, then offered a weak grip. He excused himself, saying he had to use the restroom. After washing his hands Gerard returned, and poured glasses of single-malt scotch.

It turned out the three men shared a connection. They all lived in the same community, Sarasota, Florida, although Carlos' home was a seasonal residence. He divided his time between the resort and the southwest Florida city. He and Lawson first met a few years ago at a downtown restaurant. During their initial conversation which included deep-sea fishing, Carlos had mentioned his resort. That had aroused Lawson's interest in a fishing vacation, and he traveled to Costa Rica a few times a year.

Sipping his drink and making small talk, Lawson asked Gerard what kind of work he did.

"I'm a consultant, a turnaround specialist working with companies in trouble. Years ago, when I was an attorney, I helped a few firms out. It was during a recession, and my clients were all fighting to stay alive. So, I began offering them free advice to help keep them afloat and retain them as clients. I realized I had a knack for this kind of strategic thinking. I gave up the law practice and switched to consulting full time."

"Did the consulting work out?"

"I made so much money consulting I retired to São Paulo when I was still in my forties."

"So, you're living in Sarasota now, and you're retired?"

"Not at all. After 15 years, my wife and I had it with the crime and corruption in Brazil and we moved back to the states. We selected Sarasota, and I started up my consulting gig again."

"What companies do you help? Do you focus on a specific industry?"

"My approach to problems allows me to turn around just about any company. I've helped single practitioners doing a mere $250K and mid-size firms with sales up to $10 million.

"What do you do, Ronald?"

"We market a water-saving system for housing facilities and hotels. In fact, I'm down here to supervise the team installing our equipment in Carlos' resort."

"Wow! That sounds interesting. With water shortages all over the world, it sounds like a concept that must generate millions in profits."

"Yes, that's what we expected when we founded the company. But the reality has been anything but. Even our newest breakthrough product is struggling to get traction."

At that point Carlos interrupted, saying, "Gentlemen, we've got to get over to the restaurant or we'll miss our reservation."

Later, while the men were enjoying snifters of cognac, Gerard said, "Ronald, when we get back to the states, I'd like to come by your place and look at your operation. Who knows? Maybe I can come up with some ideas and recommendations. But, only if you'd like. I don't want to impose."

"That's an unusual idea. I've never had anyone offer to help."

"Well, I usually find something you haven't thought of. I look at every challenge with a very different perspective than the owners. And that's because I have a clear mind and no pre-conceived prejudices. But, it's your call. I'm not pressuring you."

"Not at all, Gerard. I never turn down free advice. I would welcome the chance to get your views on our situation."

Later in bed, Lawson was giddy. *Gerard was impressive, a really smart guy. If he could retire in his forties, then he's got the skills to get our company on track. Bringing him in would really boost my image as CEO with the shareholders and my family.*

39

Introducing the Messiah
June 2015, Sarasota, FL

Dave Powers arrived at the office at 7:30, his calendar showing that he and Lawson were meeting with Gerard Morbus at 10. He was looking forward to hear what this consultant had to say.

When Lawson had returned from Costa Rica, he couldn't contain his excitement about the opportunity of Gerard consulting for them. Powers was getting desperate for a solution and he was ready to talk to anyone who could offer advice to help improve their situation.

It had been months since the trade show fiasco in Las Vegas, and creating a marketing message from Hedges' throwaway comment. Sales still hadn't materialized. He put up most of his remaining retirement money into the firm, and he was desperate for the company to turn profits.

Neither partner had ever drawn a salary in the seven years since they founded the company. For Powers, it was a situation he never expected, and he had been taking steps he never imagined would be necessary. Selling their home and cars to raise cash had been a traumatic experience.

It was a painful adjustment to move into a small rental home. And Powers vowed to his wife they would one day have another beautiful home on a golf course.

Lawson, fortunately, had steady income from his family trust, so money was far less important. It was much more about the perceived cachet in the eyes of his siblings and family members that he was the CEO of a thriving venture.

Thinking back a few weeks when he was told about Lawson's meeting Gerard in Costa Rica, Powers was pleasantly shocked that his partner called a meeting with this specialist. He had no idea what drove him to even consider hiring a consultant to review the firm's position and its chronic struggle for growth.

Any recommendations that Gerard could conceivably offer would usurp Lawson's authority and threaten his role as CEO. He had always jealously guarded even the appearance that he was not up to fulfilling his position as president and CEO of the company. This proved to be a troubling character trait for Powers to accept. He recognized that Lawson didn't come close to having the ability to run the company. And it showed daily.

Powers was not surprised at Lawson's lack of leadership skills. Back when his friend Sam had reviewed the initial draft of their business plan, he said Lawson should not be listed as CEO. As an investor relations expert, Sam worried that his weak bio would prove to be a negative factor in raising investment capital. And this observation proved to be accurate.

Gerard walked in at exactly 10:00. He was dressed in a tailored suit, an open-collared, custom shirt and expensive Italian shoes. Powers was impressed with the professional look he exuded. And he did not miss the fact that Gerard had parked a new S550 Mercedes Sedan right in front of their offices in the No Parking zone.

Instead of the conference room, Lawson brought them all into his large office, dimly lit with table lamps. They sat at the small conference table. Gerard looked around and said, "This place is lit like a whorehouse. Do you guys fuck broads in the back? Hahaha."

Lawson gave a perfunctory laugh, and Powers was shocked at how Gerard had just blown his well-polished image with this tasteless comment.

Gerard said he had this special gift for quickly understanding a company's problems and a long history of rapidly turning them around. He claimed that he made so much money doing this in his previous life, he retired to Brazil as a millionaire, well before he was fifty.

Getting right to the heart of the matter, Gerard asked about how the system worked; who were the end-users; what was the distribution channel. He asked about wholesale and retail pricing, manufacturing and overhead costs. He was mildly surprised when Lawson couldn't rattle off the numbers, but gave vague amounts. Powers jumped in with more accurate figures on the monthly operating costs, which were far less than expected for a company this size.

Seeing Gerard's questioning looks, Powers explained that neither of them had taken a salary since the company was founded. He also mentioned that they were both owed tens of thousands of dollars in unpaid expenses. During the entire time Gerard asked questions, he never took notes.

Now having a financial snapshot of the company, he then asked about the shareholders and the amounts of money invested. Lawson pulled out a list of investors with the number of shares each held.

Next came the big question, "So, if this product works as well as you claim, and saves 40% of a facility's water, with a three-month to six-month break-even, why isn't it selling? It should generate millions a month."

Lawson demurred, looking down at his papers. Powers fielded the question. "Any new product coming onto the housing or hospitality market with the potential to cause catastrophic damage, particularly from water, is slow to be accepted. People want proof of concept and they want the assurance that the product is safe."

"Is the product safe? Do you have substantial liability insurance?"

Lawson jumped in to show his knowledge. "Yes. It can prevent floods. And we have adequate coverage."

Powers continued, "The second problem is the installer. Plumbers are the main contractors for installation. And plumbers tend to have a left-brain mindset. They hate to change the way they do repairs and installations. Their success is based on their skill to repeat the process every day without deviation."

'Then fuck the plumbers. Do we have to sell through them?"

"It's a system requiring a plumbing installation, so there's no easy way to get around the plumbers."

"Can anybody be trained to install it? Or must it be a licensed plumber?"

"It's possible to train others, such as maintenance staff or handymen. But they probably wouldn't be as fast as plumbers.

"The key issue with plumbers is their fear that the system's efficiency will reduce future repair business. They just don't see the potential the referral business would produce from the system's performance."

Gerard's mind raced as he digested what Powers had said. "I've got the picture, so let me think about it and I will come back to you with a proposal." He ended with a few off-color jokes and left.

Following the meeting, Lawson said to Powers, "Did you see how quickly he grasped the situation? He asked all the right questions, and I bet he'll be back with a solution in no time."

Powers was not as enthusiastic as his partner but would accept a less-than-perfect white knight. The key question was if Gerard could take over Lawson's role and deliver the decision-making and leadership required of a qualified CEO.

40

A Fair Proposal

A couple of days later Gerard returned with a plan. He walked them through the steps, and with each item, Lawson became more excited, while Powers patiently absorbed the details and direction of the proposal. Gerard articulated the key barriers that were holding the company back. He emphasized the rejection by the plumbers and the lack of testimonial proof.

Conversely, he pointed out the growing issue with water shortages around the country, particularly the Southwest. And he was confident, with a high-powered salesperson working with him, they could sell truckloads of systems.

The biggest area of concern was funding, and Gerard also had a solution for that. His recommendation was a reverse stock split. All the shareholders would maintain their same proportion of stock but at a lower share value. They could then sell more shares, and raise the capital to grow.

Lawson sat there, giddy, knowing that he was the one who brought in the savior. Meanwhile, Powers asked about Gerard's terms of engagement.

"My compensation is always back-end loaded because the companies I work for are broke. If I don't produce, I don't earn. So, you're protected from me skimming money without results."

Powers asked, "What would your income be when we turn the corner?"

"Initially, I will raise capital, and take 5% of the funds raised. I will not receive any compensation until we are profitable, and then we will all take a salary. But I will also receive a 5% share of stock when we sell the company."

Lawson blurted out, "It sounds like we've got a deal." But Powers interjected, "I think we need more information before we commit. First, even with a fire-breathing sales rep, how can you succeed when we have failed for so long?"

"Easy, we're going to do the installations directly with hotels and apartment buildings. Once we have a track record of marquee properties, we will train the maintenance teams at large facilities to do their own installs."

Powers replied, "I'm not comfortable with that because it creates a serious liability issue. Our insurance premiums will balloon. But I won't rule it out just yet."

"Higher insurance premiums are no problem if we're selling large quantities of systems."

"Agreed. Now, what about your credentials? Do you have references? Which customers have you successfully revived?"

"I've turned around a few companies right here in town. But you can't call them right now, as I'm winding down my services with them. I don't want them thinking I may leave before my work is done. Your company is going to require my full attention, so I won't be able to continue with any of these firms."

"How about the clients you served before you came here?"

"That was 15 years ago. I'm sure none of them are still in business."

Lawson jumped in. "My friend Carlos from the resort spoke very highly of Gerard, so I'm comfortable with him. I like the plan."

Ignoring him, he continued, "Gerard, you outlined your terms, but what are your rules of engagement? How do we track your performance? And how do you interface with Ronald and me?"

"Good questions, Dave. Think of this as a new company. I hate to say it, but you two have failed. I have to rebuild this operation from the ground up. As I mentioned, the stock is worthless, but you earn more stock to keep ahead of the other investors."

Confused, Powers asked, "How will we do that?"

"Easy. We will set aside a block of stock to reward the management team for performance."

"And how will we distribute the management responsibilities?"

"I will be in complete charge. I will be both CEO and Board Chairman. And I will make all the decisions. Now that may sound harsh, but in these situations, the rescue team usually fires the entire management staff and restructures the company. We may not have to do that. Are we all in agreement on how we will proceed?"

Powers was aware that Lawson's enthusiasm quickly went from excited to depressed. You could hear the air escaping from his balloon. He thought this was a good move. He knew it was critical to get his partner out of the CEO position, and he was willing to take a chance on Gerard. He turned to his Lawson, "You still okay with this?"

Putting his partner on the spot, Powers wasn't surprised when Lawson's answer was a very feeble, "Well, I guess so."

41

Changing Job Descriptions

The next morning, Gerard swept into the office like a hurricane. He brought a two-page agreement that outlined the simple terms they had discussed, and asked Lawson and Powers to sign it. "Our first objective is increasing funds. So, we're going to call a shareholders meeting right away. Anyone who lives in town can come to the office, and the others will teleconference in."

Turning to Lawson, Gerard asked, "Can you arrange a meeting with your wealthy brother, the one you mentioned in Costa Rica who runs your family's business? Let's consult with him and see if he has any ideas about making the firm grow faster. And when he hears our plan, I bet he will want to invest."

The idea interested Lawson, as he would like nothing better than to have his big brother involved in this venture. While he didn't want his family to know that he was no longer the CEO of the company, discussing the possibilities on the same level as his brother would reflect well on him.

Later, when Lawson left for a meeting with the family's bank trustee, Powers sat with Gerard to talk about some sales leads. After that, Gerard mentioned to him that if Lawson could not get his brother to invest, then he was of no use to the company. "I'll cut him loose if he can't deliver. Without a source of funds, there is no other way he can help us. He's just dead weight."

"Not true, Gerard. You're overlooking the one value that he possesses. His family belongs to the yacht club and two country clubs. He is well connected in the Sarasota community. And he can strike up a conversation with anyone. He opens a lot of leads with important prospects."

"Dave, don't insult my intelligence. This flawed thinking has cost you your company. We can't afford to keep someone in a top management position just because he can bullshit with some influential strangers. So, if he can't deliver, he's off the fucking ranch."

42

Thanks, But No Thanks

A week later, Lawson brought his brother Royce to the office to meet with Gerard. Royce was in Sarasota to visit his mother and enjoy one of his frequent vacations. He wore Tommy Bahama slacks and a Sarasota Yacht Club monogrammed shirt. A taller, somewhat older version of his brother, he shared the same smile. Royce seemed enthused to be invited to share his expertise on helping the company.

The four men met around the conference table as Gerard explained the company's key issues. Royce listened intently, took notes and offered a very good suggestion. "The one thing that I learned about hotels and apartment buildings, is to talk directly with the owner or general manager. Don't bother with maintenance staff or property managers. They can't make the decisions and don't want to take on any extra work."

Gerard asked Royce if he would invest in the company. "We're looking for a couple of investors to put up a mere $250,000 each."

Royce politely declined, so Gerard pushed back, asking if he would consider a tranche of $100,000 to help his brother. Royce's clarified response was, "I'm not at all interested in any investment in HydroDyne now."

He seemed miffed at being pressured to invest as he did not expect they would solicit him at this meeting. He had no clue that the request might be part of the discussion. Royce packed away his note pad, and stood to leave. He asked to use the men's room, and while he was in there, Gerard turned to Powers and whispered, "Do I have to shake his hand? What if he doesn't wash his hands after he pees?"

Shocked he answered, "Of course, you do. What the hell's the matter with you?"

As Royce left, they all shook hands. Gerard, however, did so with much trepidation. He hurried to thoroughly wash his hands.

When Lawson walked Royce out to his car, Gerard looked at Powers and shrugged his shoulders. After he returned to the conference room, Gerard chided him, "Ronald, I can't believe Royce refused to put up even $100K to help his kid brother. What kind of family do you have? And why didn't you ask him? Why wait for me to hit him up?"

In one of those rare instances, Lawson grew incensed. He barked at Gerard, "You have no idea about my family's financial relationships. Why didn't you tell me you were going to ask him for money? I would have stopped you. Do you know how embarrassing that was for me?"

"Embarrassed? You stupid fuck. Your company is going down the shitter, and you're afraid to ask your brother for money because it might make you look bad. Why do you think we invited him over?"

Lawson stormed to his office and sat there brooding. Gerard walked to the front office and started reviewing the books.

After lunch, Gerard called them back into the conference room. Gerard addressed Lawson, who seemed to have regained his composure. "Ronald, I just did a cursory review of the books, and they are one fucking mess. I can't tell a thing from them."

"Look, I'm not a bookkeeper. What do you expect?"

"Hey, I'm not a bookkeeper either. Fuck, I hate looking at spreadsheets, but I can see that the accounts are screwed up. Nothing balances, and there's no inventory. How do you even know how much you are losing each month?

"Anyway, you won't be keeping the books any longer. I'll bring in a real bookkeeper to straighten out the books and they will be kept accurately.

"And Ronald, since we all have to be productive, I have a new challenge for you. Dave tells me that you are connected through the social hubs in town and have a knack for striking up conversations."

Puffing up, Lawson said, "Yeah. I know the movers and shakers in town. And I can talk to anyone."

"Here's what we're going to do. You hang around the clubs. Find out who makes the decisions at the condo buildings, who serves on the boards, who owns apartment buildings and hotels."

"I know some of them. They're members of the yacht club."

"Great. Also, go to the hotel lounges, and meet the management staff. Let them know your company can save them a ton of money by saving water. Just get the leads, prepare a weekly report, and then Dave will close the deals. Think you can handle that?"

"Sure. I've been doing some of that already. I'm working on a couple right now, and have appointments."

"Super. But take Dave with you and let him do the closing. He has more sales experience. And listen carefully, Ronald. If you can't handle this assignment, I don't know where else I can put you. So, don't disappoint me. Capiche?"

43

Declining the Job Offer

Gerard was eating a late lunch at one of his favorite daytime restaurants with his favorite waitress. He often came in for either breakfast or lunch. And he always tried to pick a table that was covered by a server he liked named Angie.

She was cute, with a lavender streak in her blonde hair. She had a thin frail body, almost emaciated. Gerard always thought it might be from drug use. He once referred to her as having a negative 32AA bra size. He liked the way she always flirted.

When he finished his cheddar cheese sandwich with lettuce, she brought him his check and made some small talk, "How's it going, Mr. G? What's new?"

"Always good, Angie. A new consulting gig that is challenging. But it's going to be a huge win for me. The company has enormous potential."

And whispering, she asked, "Any chance you need a part-time worker? I get off at two every day, and I need to make more."

"Matter of fact, I just let the girl in the front office go. What are your office skills? Can you do bookkeeping?"

"I'm not a bookkeeper, but I've done entries and posting in QuickBooks. I have computer skills and I can do other office stuff."

He handed her the address. "Come over after work today, and let's talk about how you can help me."

Touching his shoulder, she answered, "Thank you, Mr. G. I'll see you later. I promise you won't be sorry."

126

When she showed up, Gerard took her into his office to talk. She had changed after work and was wearing a tight skirt that came less than halfway down her tanned thighs, and a tee-shirt under her blouse.

"Angie, I just took over this company, and the books and records are a mess. If you can catch up with the posting and keep the books, I'll pay you better than the going rate. If you work out, I'll have the accountant train you on the more advanced bookkeeping and reporting."

"Mr. G, that sounds great. Where do I start?"

"First, call me Gerard in the office. Now let's go out front and straighten out the filing. Take all the piles of papers on top of the cabinets, organize them, and load them into the file cabinets. I'm in my office if you have any questions."

"Is it okay if I play some music? It's like a morgue in this place."

"Yes. Just keep it down. And none of that ghetto music, you know, rap. I hate that shit. And besides, this is a place of business."

The two of them were alone in the office all afternoon. At 6 pm, Gerard walked out front to check on Angie. She organized most of the clutter.

She was bent over, loading folders into a file cabinet. The back of her tiny skirt was so high, it revealed her bikini panties.

Gerard gasped silently. "Wow, Angie. You have great thighs."

She straightened up and turned to him with a nervous smile. "I'm sorry. I should dress differently in here."

With a lecherous grin he answered, "No, you're fine. Just don't let anyone else see your crotch but me. This place is looking great. Why don't you work another half-hour and then let's talk?"

Later, Gerard was sitting on his couch with papers scattered around him. Gathering them up, he told her to sit down. "Angie, the front office looks so much better. If you can do this much work every day, I'll pay you $20 an hour.

And in a month, once you know the office, I'll raise you to $25."

She jumped with a shriek. "Oh, Gerard, thank you so much!"

She hugged him. He pushed her back and gave her a wet kiss, as he forced his tongue into her mouth. When she pulled away, he said, "Now, how about a blow job?"

Quickly standing up, she blurted, "Are you fucking crazy? You low-life sleaze bag! I thought you were serious about me working for you. I'm out of here."

She grabbed her purse and raced out the door. Gerard yelled to her back, "What the fuck's the matter with you, you dumb twat? This is how it happens in an office. With that attitude, you'll be stuck in that shitty, coffee-shop job the rest of your life."

44

Racially-Charged Termination

At the weekly update meeting, Lawson reported several prospective properties, along with names of members and chairs of condo boards, and the GM of a large downtown hotel.

Surprised, Gerard said, "If you can do this every week, we'll have more local business than we ever imagined. Dave, get with Ronald and follow up with appointments for these people. Let's close a deal quickly."

That afternoon, Gerard met with Johnson Park, the firm's engineer who developed the flagship product. Gerard asked him about his education and told him about his plan to install the system in multifamily properties. In trying to engage Johnson, he joked about his heritage. "Johnson, how old are you? I could never guess the age of Chinese people."

Irritated, he responded, "I am not Chinese. Everyone knows that Park is one of the most popular Korean names in the world. And I'm 30."

"Well, you're pretty young to be an engineer with a patent pending. But here's what I'm thinking. Since we're a tiny company, and you're the only one who knows this system intimately, I want you to take over the install process when we get our first orders."

"I'm an engineer, not a mechanic. I won't be an installer. I'm really busy, designing a new product, and some upgrades. You can hire a plumber or a technician for the installs."

"Johnson, this is only temporary. You know the system. I don't have to train you to install. You can do it tomorrow.

And after we get going, you can train other techs to do that work."

"I'll think about it."

"You'll think about it? Listen you fucking Chink. You'll either take the assignment, or get the fuck out."

"Then I'm done. I'll pack up and be out of here today. And my attorney is going to salivate when he hears that you called me a 'fucking Chink'."

"Good luck with that. It's your word against mine, and I'm a lawyer. So, who's the judge going to believe?"

45

Another Bone Yard Candidate

On the same day that Johnson walked out, Gerard texted Paul Hedges and asked him to meet the next morning.

Hedges arrived at his usual time, thinking he would attend a board meeting. He was surprised to learn that Gerard was the only one in the office. Introducing himself, he said, "Hi, I'm Paul Hedges, and you are Gerard Morbus? Where is everyone?"

Gerard pointed to a chair opposite his desk. "Everyone is out making sales calls and trying to grow the business. What have you done for the company?"

"I've been an invaluable member of the board. Just my name on the record has enabled most of the investment money the company has received."

Surprised by his brazenness, Gerard interrupted, "Are you fucking kidding me? Can you name one person who invested because you're a board member? And can your gold-plated name raise any more money? We sure could use it now. Just how much did you invest, Mr. Hedge Fund, or whatever your fucking name is?"

Stammering, Hedges tried to defend himself by saying, "No one will invest now. The company's in shambles. And without me, it would have gone down much sooner. I've been the one responsible for keeping Ronald and Dave on the straight and narrow."

"Look, you fucking wanker, they do not need a parole officer, certainly Dave doesn't. What we do need is sales and an infusion of cash. So how much are you going to invest?"

"I wouldn't invest a shilling in this place. It will not make it."

"In that case, turn in your fucking stock, that's not worth a shilling, and you didn't pay for, and get the fuck out!"

With his face trembling and his hands shaking, Hedges stood up and said, "You can't talk to me like that, I'm a board member. And I earned that stock and will not give it back. Morbus, you are a vile man."

"And you, Hedger, are off the fucking board as of now. And if you don't turn in your stock, you will find out just how vile I am."

46

The Lockout

At the next informal Friday sales meeting. Powers reported he had two appointments, and was confirming a few others. He also had a response from a hotel in Vancouver to an email promotion he ran a few months prior. Gerard told him not to bother with hotels in Canada as the Pacific Northwest had far above average rainfalls, and there would be no interest in a water-saving system.

Powers ignored the comments.

When Lawson handed over his list, Gerard scanned it. He shouted: "What the fuck is this? These are the same names you handed in last week."

"That isn't true. There are two new ones this week."

"And you think getting two new names is productive? I could get two names in an hour, just by cold calling. When we meet next week, you had better have a dozen new prospects on that fucking list, or don't even bother to show up."

Lawson stormed out. He was uncomfortable around Gerard, and didn't know how to handle it. He had never faced serious confrontation or ridicule in his sheltered life. He felt like he was being berated constantly and could not deal with Gerard's verbal abuse. Lawson didn't remember him being like that in Costa Rica. He grew convinced that Gerard had a split personality.

After the meeting, Powers followed up Gerard's request for a locksmith to change all the building's locks. With Johnson, Hedges and the front desk clerk gone, he didn't want any of the terminated staff having access.

Late that afternoon, the locksmith showed up to change all the locks. It took him an hour and he gave a couple sets of keys to Powers. A short time after he left, Powers locked up and went home for the weekend.

The next morning while playing golf, his wife Elisa got a call at home from Lawson looking for Powers. Hearing his agitation, she asked, "Ronald, is everything okay?"

"No, Elisa. Nothing is okay. I went to the office to get some tools that I keep stored in the warehouse, and my key didn't work. Gerard and Dave changed the locks to keep me out. I'm so pissed."

"Wait a minute, Ronald. I don't know what the problem is between you and Gerard, but Dave thinks he is doing a good job. I don't know anything about the locks, but Dave would never intentionally lock you out."

He shouted, "See, you're still taking his side. It was deliberate. And I know it."

"Look, Ronald, if you're going to act like a child, then don't come to us for sympathy." She hung up and then called Powers on his cell, leaving a message.

At the nine-hole turn, Powers checked his messages and called her back. She was still livid at Lawson's treatment of her and she explained what he had said. Powers told her he would call him after his round of golf.

Before he came home, Powers reached Lawson and blasted him. "Don't you ever raise your voice to my wife. Who do you think you are? Say anything you want to me, but leave her out of it. Are we clear?"

"But she was taking Gerard's side. You changed the locks to keep me out."

"I changed the locks yesterday afternoon at Gerard's request. I didn't think it would matter to you. Except for yesterday's meeting, you haven't been to the office in over a week. Besides, I'm always the first one there in the morning. There's a set of keys on your desk."

Lawson never approached the building again.

47

Building the Team

Walking into the conference room for their Friday meeting, Gerard said to Powers, "I guess it just got too hot in the whorehouse for Ronald."

"What? What is that supposed to mean?"

"I knew he'd take off as soon as his job got to be work of any kind. So now the only ones left are the adults, you and me."

"Well, we're going to need a few more adults if we're going to grow this company. We can't do it alone."

"I just hired a good bookkeeper who I've worked with in the past. Her name is Amanda Rolle. She will come in part-time, do the books and handle the phones. I also called our corporate attorney and asked her to come in for a meeting, although I don't expect to keep her. She is a woman, after all."

Frustrated by Gerard, Powers asked, "How could you say that without even meeting her? You know nothing about her and you already want to get rid of her? I don't get it."

"Look, if she were a good lawyer, she wouldn't be in this small resort town. She would be in Miami or Atlanta. And on top of that, she's a woman. We don't need a domesticated broad, we need a shark."

"I don't agree. We're keeping her. She's board-certified and she's that good. She also has experience working for a publicly-held company."

"Lest you forget, I decide around here. But, if you feel that strongly, I will give her the benefit of the doubt. I'll hold off on my decision until I meet her, and she impresses me."

"You are the decision-maker. But don't expect me to stand by when you make the wrong call. I've been in business far longer than you, and I've got lots of experience in many industries. So, expect pushback from time to time. It's healthy and it's good because you don't always have the right answers."

Although he backed off, Gerard was not used to anyone standing up to him or having his directives distrusted. And he knew this would be a problem down the road. Powers was a smart guy, but Gerard would have to make him compliant and not question his authority and his decisions.

When Barbara Newman came into the office, Gerard was impressed. She wore an expensive dark blue suit with a lavender silk blouse. She was very tall, about five-foot, seven, full-figured with a pleasant face. In explaining her background, Newman was self-confident, smart, and experienced. He could quickly see that by her no-nonsense attitude that she was comfortable functioning in a man's world and not easily intimidated.

He also learned that she had a strong background in corporate law and certifications in business litigation and professional liability. He liked that her blouse was open to the point of revealing a deep cleavage from her rounded breasts.

Gerard filled her in on the developments that had taken place over the last few weeks. And he told her he was about to execute his plan for a reverse stock split. She advised him to schedule a board meeting right away and get everything on the agenda and approved. She explained that due process was critical in companies of this structure.

He appreciated her comments, as that concept hadn't even occurred to him. This was the first company he ran that was registered with multiple shareholders. She could be a valuable resource, and he suggested she serve on the board that he was restructuring.

48

Orders from a Higher Authority

Powers was pleased to win his skirmish with Gerard and was feeling more comfortable pushing to keep Newman hired with Gerard's change of heart. With her on the board, he had an ally to support him in the event of a serious disagreement with Gerard.

The order came in from the hotel in Canada, and Powers discussed the installation steps with its maintenance chief, who concluded the process was not difficult, and he had the blessing of the hotel's director to take on the project.

When told about the order, Gerard was fuming. He said to Powers, "I told you not to take that order."

"You said we need sales and we need them fast. This is the biggest order we've had in six months. And it's a major chain hotel in Canada that could lead to dozens of other properties in the franchise."

"We can't handle one hotel a couple of thousand miles away in another country."

"They're doing their own installation. They could be on the moon, and I'd sell them the system."

"But you went rogue on me."

"If you want me to follow your orders, you have to be consistent. I'm a leader and I'm good at making decisions."

Although Powers was right again, this was another small blemish on his record in Gerard's mind. He was used to people buckling when he bullied them. And that's the only way he knew how to manage.

Later that day, Gerard came in to Powers' office with a copy of an email that the bookkeeper passed on to him.

"Who is this Green Solutions company in Indiana?"

"That's our oldest distributor. It's a small company, but we get orders from them every month."

"Well, I want you to fire them. They just placed an order and their last month's payment is late. Their communication is also very unprofessional. Their email has some reference to God printed under the signature."

"You're contradicting yourself, again. The owner is an ordained minister with a huge following. And printing an innocuous psalm on his emails is no reason to turn down his steady business."

"We don't do business with religious fanatics."

"He's not a fanatic. He considers ecology part of his mission and gets his business through his congregation. Occasionally, his payment is a couple of weeks late."

'So, what's with the God reference?"

"We will not stop doing business with one of our steadiest customers, because you're troubled by a religious quote on his emails. Do you want to have to explain that to the shareholders? I didn't think so."

And once again, Powers bruised Gerard's fragile ego. To soothe his anger, Powers offered, "I'll get a check from him before we ship the next order."

The following morning Gerard came into the office after he made the bank deposit. He said, "I just met the bank branch manager, who has great tits, by the way. She told me her husband is a property manager, and he wants to get back into a sales position. He's coming in tomorrow for an interview."

"Sounds excellent. You said you wanted someone strong who can devote their full effort to sales. Let's hope he's good."

"She told me he was a top sales rep for a distributor before he took the property manager's position."

"Coincidently, I've been working on a redesign of the website. With the installation services, we must include technical information and an installation video."

"Don't waste your time with the website. Nobody reads them. It's all about sales."

Powers was incredulous, but he knew better than to say a word in response. He would figure out how to get the website upgraded without another confrontation with Gerard.

49

Serious Flaw Exposed

Emilio Lopez arrived at nine the next morning. He was young, tall, and good looking. His premature gray temples contrasted with his jet-black hair and striking blue-gray eyes. Emilio was born and raised in Cuba where he worked in building construction starting at age 16. He emigrated to Miami, and used his knowledge to land a sales position at a construction materials distributor. His customer base consisted of property managers and maintenance directors at condos and hotels in the Miami area.

One of Emilio's top clients was the owner of a large portfolio of apartment buildings. Influenced by the way Emilio helped his team with recommendations and advice, the owner offered him a management position. Emilio accepted and studied for his property manager's license. Soon after he took the management position, he realized that this was not the career for him. He yearned to be back in sales.

Gerard and Powers were both impressed with Emilio, and sensed his selling skills. They were both ready to make an offer that day.

Emilio asked about the system, the pricing, and the documented results. Satisfied with the product, he moved to the marketing support and asked about what the plan included. Gerard responded before Powers. "Don't worry about the marketing. We're sales driven, and this system is so good, it will sell itself."

"No offense, Mr. Morbus, but nothing sells itself. You said we need sales quickly. A marketing program is essential. And your website is outdated. That will hurt credibility, and make sales more difficult."

Powers was about to respond, but Gerard waved him off, and replied, "Don't worry about the website. Nobody reads websites."

The mood changed immediately as Emilio realized that Gerard was a marketing neophyte. And in his mind, he was rejecting the company as a potential employer. Closing his briefcase, he prepared to end the interview by saying, "Let me think this over and I'll get back to you."

At that point, Powers jumped in. "Emilio, my key role in the company is marketing, and I am a nationally recognized expert. I have a plan that we will implement shortly. I'm working on an updated website, which I can show you."

"Yes, I would like to see what you're doing. Both are important."

"I agree with your thinking, and you will get all the support you need. We're expecting additional investment funding, and some of that will go for the marketing effort."

"Well, it's a relief to hear that. Without a program to create interest in the system, I would waste my time. Will the website upgrades have to wait for the funds that you mentioned?"

Looking to Gerard for tacit approval, which didn't come, Powers said, "The website will only cost one or two thousand. That will be completed quickly."

Feeling better about the opportunity, Emilio ended on an upbeat note, saying, "You have a breakthrough system that will change water consumption, and I want to be part of it. I think I can contribute in a big way. I look forward to our next meeting."

As soon as Emilio was out the door, Gerard shouted at Powers, "What the fuck is the matter with you? Why did you tell him we're going ahead with any of that shit? We don't have time for marketing."

"I just kept you from making a fool of yourself. He was ready to walk. If you didn't see that, then you have no interview skills. He knows what he needs to be successful. He did his homework and he knew the website is dated. You have to admit that I just changed his mind about going with us."

"Bullshit! I would have closed him."

"And you would have failed. You keep contradicting yourself. A good marketing program accelerates sales. It doesn't slow the effort. If you would have said that to him, he would have got up and walked out regardless of what I told him. So, let's get the website updated, and launch a marketing program when we have the cash. Learn to trust me, particularly when it comes to marketing."

Gerard was shown that he was wrong again, yet had to accept that Powers had deftly saved the situation. He wanted Emilio on board, and without admitting it, it was a sure bet that he would have walked.

"Tell you what. If he takes the job, you've got $2,000 to spend on the website. And never contradict me again in front of anyone."

"I was careful not to contradict you. He didn't know what we discussed. I just worked around your misguided directives, and I salvaged a recruit that we both want. We're a team, right? We're the adults in the room, right? So, swallow your pride and be glad for what we just accomplished."

Powers walked back to his office troubled by the recent events and what just transpired. How could Gerard be so naive about the benefits of marketing? Could he have ever turned around any company without some amount of marketing support? He must pay closer attention to Gerard's decisions.

Gerard sat at his desk thinking about his latest altercation with Powers. There was no question he was a leader, and he was smart. But Gerard had to use his knowledge and control him or he would have to jettison him from the company. No one defied him and survived.

50

Confronting the Truth

The following week turned out to be one of the best weeks in the company's history, one that solidified Gerard's position as the savior CEO.

On Monday, Emilio accepted the sales position, and he brought in a test order from a huge prospect. Before taking the job, he contacted a friend in Miami and told him about the system. The timing couldn't be better, as the facility had been ordered by its board to reduce recurring costs. If the system proved effective, it would result in a series of installs across the country for the hundreds of properties owned by the real estate investment trust.

That same afternoon, Norman from Green Solutions in Indiana sent in the largest single order HydroDyne had ever received. When Powers showed the order to Gerard, he said, "I thought you fired that company."

"I told you I would not terminate them. They are too important a client."

"How are they going to pay?"

"Due to the size of the order, Norman asked his client for a substantial upfront deposit. Green Solutions' account is now current, and they will prepay part of this order."

Gerard was delighted with the order, particularly the timing. Once again, he was annoyed his demands had been ignored. Powers sat there without emotion as Gerard berated him about not following orders. It was as if he were being scolded by a first-grade teacher.

Misconstruing how the repetition was affecting Powers' attention span, Gerard shouted, "Are you fucking zoning out on me? You pay attention when I talk. Do you hear?"

"If you expect me to pay attention to what you're saying, then treat *me* with respect. I have very good listening skills and a superior IQ. Say it once, not ten times."

"Don't give me that shit. I've had to address this issue with you a dozen times already. So now, I'm going to repeat it until you get it."

"Gerard, as smart as you are, you just don't get that we have different areas of expertise, and they complement each other. I have launched over 20 companies in my career."

"That just means you had 19 failures, and this will be number 20. Hahaha."

"Yes. I've had some failures, but that's how you learn and grow. No one succeeds without failures. If I sit back and let you screw up, then you'll have a major failure on your hands. Maybe then you'll appreciate my advice."

Powers stood, collected his paperwork to return to his office.

"Don't you fucking walk out on me. I'm not finished with you."

"I've been listening to you say nothing productive for the past half hour. Now you listen. You demand respect, but you have none for anyone. You are a brilliant strategist, but your execution is like a clumsy juggler."

"What the fuck are you talking about?"

"There are areas where I'm smarter than you, and I have lots more experience than you. I have consulted for brilliant people running huge corporations. Together, we have the smarts to make this company wildly successful. But your pride and ego are holding you back."

Powers stood and walked out. Gerard was not used to being confronted by the truth. He paced around the office deciding what to do with him. *I don't care how smart he is, I have to get rid of him. Nobody questions my authority.*

51

Impressing the Shareholders

The shareholder meeting was held on Thursday morning and it allowed Gerard to boast about the sales activity. He gave the investors the impression that he was solely responsible for the recent spurt of orders. This stroke of good timing put everyone in a positive mood, leading up to the request for them to make an additional investment.

In presenting his pitch, Gerard seemed nervous. The shareholders noticed. Sensing that there was some apprehension among the investors regarding Gerard, Powers jumped into the prepared remarks and spoke up. He praised Gerard's foresight to move from plumbing distribution to the direct installation model. He pointed out that sales had jumped dramatically and the pipeline for new business was expanding beyond expectations.

This reinforcement that Gerard was the right choice to lead the company pushed the investors over the top. Gerard noticed it. Instead of appreciating this show of support, he worried that Powers had the trust, respect and admiration of all the investors.

As the meeting progressed, one asked Powers about the now obsolete website. Before he could respond, Gerard answered, "We've already started work on it."

Another asked what was the company going to do with the new capital it raised, beyond covering overhead. Powers answered this one, "With our growth targets, we'll need additional funds for marketing, plus any additional sales-related expenses." This drew nods from all present and a comment from Tommy Cantarella, one of the larger shareholders. "That sounds great. It's about time we devoted some money to marketing."

After answering all the questions, Gerard described his plan to reward anyone who brought in new investors and increased their capital position with bonus shares of stock. This incentive helped raise $350,000 in new investment funds.

Following the meeting, Gerard strolled into Powers' office.

He said, "Dave, when we restructured, I kept you and got rid of the others. And I made the right decision. You have the experience and a confident speaking style. I saw how those investors listened to you, and sought your tacit approval. We are going to make a great team and we're going to get rich together. But I have the final say. There can only be one person in charge. So, keep that in mind, and let's make it work."

Gerard walked back to his office, and Powers sat there wondering if this change of heart was fleeting or permanent. It was a small victory, but he recognized that coming from Gerard it was a big deal.

As he thought back, he had now reached the right decision on every single controversy against Gerard. These included the lawyer, Newman, salvaging the interview with Emilio, and also the firm's client relationship with Norman from Green Solutions. His push for the new website and a marketing program won over both Emilio and the investors. And his acceptance of the big order from the Vancouver hotel had already led to two additional hotels in western Canada ordering the product.

It made him question Gerard's abilities. Was he the strategic visionary he claimed, or merely a tactical turnaround pretender used to consulting with small, single-practitioner operations? He seemed to be on the wrong side of any long-range or in-depth challenges.

Powers decided, going forward he would pay much closer attention to Gerard's decisions, and be ready to stand up to him whenever he felt that his CEO was wrong.

52

Perception is Reality

Gerard told Salete he was taking her on a special date on Saturday night. They went to the Ritz Carlton, had a few drinks at the bar, and sat at a table overlooking the bay and the inlet. The sun was setting behind St. Armand's Circle on the barrier island across Sarasota Bay. The reflection off the water and the cumulous clouds provided a magnificent show of brilliant color that changed constantly until dark. Gerard ordered a $130 bottle of Moet champagne with their first course.

When the champagne was poured, she asked, "What is celebration about?"

He handed her a check for $17,500. "This is my fee for having raised $350,000. Wait until next week and then you can deposit it in our money market account. And expect that there will be more checks like that coming in. This company is about to take off, and I'm going to make a fortune."

She smiled. "This is good news. I am very much happy for you. For me, it is not so good. It not easy to get customers. They are not wanting my services. Is it because they see me as Hispanic?"

"I didn't think of that. There are a lot of wealthy people in Sarasota, but some are very prejudiced, especially those snobby WASPs. They don't see an affluent, successful woman of Brazilian heritage. Instead, they think you are an illegal from Mexico."

"I am upset about my business. It is depressing that I have trouble getting orders from rich people with no taste.

They look at me like housecleaner. I will give up this business."

"Salete, it's okay if you don't work. We now have plenty of money, and I will be making more than we ever had."

53

Firing Back

When Powers completed the website design work, he sent the files over to Computer Systems, Inc. to begin the upgrade. He and owner Joe Floret had a long history. They worked together on many projects going back over a dozen years. Powers asked for expedited service, as he wanted to get the new site up in about two weeks.

After he placed the order, he sent Gerard and Emilio an email confirming the website project was underway. Gerard, seeing the email, asked Amanda for the contact information.

That afternoon Powers drove to Gainesville on a sales call, and from there, went to Jacksonville to spend a couple of days meeting with a distributor and some of their prospects. While he was gone, Gerard called Joe Floret.

"Is this Floret? I'm Gerard Morbus. I'm the new CEO and board chairman at HydroDyne. I don't know how you worked with Powers in the past, but from now on, I'm in charge, and I'm the one who makes all the decisions."

"Well, Mr. Morbus, I'm delighted to hear you have taken over the reins of the company. However, I don't know you, and the order is signed by Dave Powers. I've worked with him for years, and he understands the web development process. Do you have any experience directing and specifying website development? I..."

Interrupting him, Gerard shouted, "Look, Floret. I told you I'm in charge here. Powers doesn't know what he's doing, especially with marketing. You work with me from now on."

"I think we have a disconnect here, sir. Dave is one of the brightest marketing guys I've ever known, and I'm in the business over 20 years. And if we're going to communicate, you will never badmouth him to me again. Am I clear?"

"Powers doesn't know a fucking thing about marketing. He doesn't even know it's a complete waste of time. It's all about sales."

"I warned you not to badmouth Dave. I'm canceling the order, but since we already started the project, I'm not refunding your deposit. And you, Mr. Superman, if you can figure out how to get out of the phone booth, you can get your own website done. You must be the dumbest asshole on the planet."

When he hung up, Gerard was probably the closest he had ever come to having a stroke. Unable to control his rage, he sent a text to Powers that read, "You're Fired!!!"

At the same time the text came in, Joe Floret called him and filled him in on his conversation with Gerard. Powers was angry with Gerard's behavior. He thanked Joe and told him that he had handled the situation the right way. He was now on his way to Jacksonville, so he pulled over and responded to Gerard's text:

Rethink this stupid directive. I don't respond to threats. I have the shareholders on my side. And you don't want a pissing contest about marketing. If they find out how little you know they will fire your ass. Talk when I get back.

When he got the text, Gerard's neck and face turned red. He sat cursing and throwing pens and paper clips around. Amanda had been getting ready to leave for the day, when she heard his tantrum. She tried to calm him down. His veins were bulging in his neck. Becoming alarmed, she went around his desk, took his hand, and tried to soothe him. He told her, "You have no fucking idea how hard it is to deal with these immature idiots. They act like children."

"Gerard, don't talk. Just take slow, deep breaths."

She put her hand on his chest and could feel his heart pounding like a jackhammer. Scared for him, now, she began massaging his chest and the back of his neck. Gerard then pulled her onto his lap and put his head in her chest. He calmed down. As he relaxed, he kissed her breasts through her top. She pulled back slightly. "Gerard, we can't be doing this. You need to go home and rest. And you need to do it now, before you have a stroke. I am very afraid for you. I'll lock up."

Gerard went home and got into bed. He was physically and emotionally exhausted from the outrageous pushback from Powers. *How dare he threaten me?* He spent the next day in bed. Too embarrassed to let Amanda know he was in bed, he texted her he was going to Miami to work with Emilio. He was also unprepared for his confrontation with Powers.

54

Shuffling the Deck

Returning to the office on Thursday, Powers was ready to confront Gerard. It was early and he could conduct some research. He went online and looked up Gerard Morbus, attorney in California. And despite going back 25 years on every attorney directory he could find, there was no lawyer ever listed. So, who was Gerard Morbus?

When Amanda arrived, Powers asked her when Gerard was expected. She explained he had gone to Miami to work with Emilio, and wouldn't be back until Monday.

Following his clash with Powers, Gerard spent the weekend strategizing his change in plan. When he became CEO, he had decided that Powers was the only employee from the original firm that he would keep. It was in his best interest to purge the rest so he'd have total control. Knowing it would raise flags with all the investors if he forced a mass exodus, he chose Powers to be the one to keep.

He had thought he could manage him, based on his easy style, but he underestimated his toughness and resolve. He had stood his ground and fought back on every directive given to him.

Now, to marginalize him, he would have to take a few steps, starting with changing his responsibilities. He then had to get him off the board, and finally he would tarnish Powers' image among the shareholders.

As soon as Gerard arrived on Monday morning, he called Powers into his office. Acting like the previous week's tensions never happened, he announced that there would be a slight restructure. "I've been thinking about your need for compensation and my promise to the shareholders that we would not be getting paid until the company is profitable.

"I called the attorney and I'm changing your status to a sales rep on commission. I will also pay you for any marketing projects you undertake. But I must take you off the board otherwise the investors will think you're getting special treatment. They still blame you for the collapse of the company."

Since Powers had not had a paycheck since the founding of the firm, he was pleased and relieved about earning some income. He also noted Gerard's dig about the shareholders' blaming him for their plight. While it bothered him, he felt confident that most of them considered him the one who kept the company afloat.

His mind was racing. He worried about leaving the board. He did not want Gerard to have unfettered power. He'd talk with Newman so they would both recommend the same investor as a replacement for him.

Gerard continued, "Here's the way we'll handle the sales. You make calls on any prospects that you think are viable. Emilio will follow up on your prospects and conclude the deals. You spend all your time generating leads and get a 5% commission on each sale closed. And you'll still be eligible for your year-end bonus of 10,000 shares.

"For any marketing projects, we'll pay you $75 per hour. I'll start with the website, but we're not using that jerkoff Floret. He is the most disrespectful prick I have ever dealt with. I found another website developer and he'll do the project using your creative direction and my approval."

As part of his plan, Gerard offered Newman a salaried position with the company. She had lost a couple of large clients recently. Recalling that she had once been managing partner at a law firm, he tailored a deal for her to become a part-time office administrator. She would also get her standard hourly rate for any legal services she provided for the company.

This enabled her to keep all her major clients and also have a steady income source. She was thrilled with her new arrangement, as her income from her law practice had shrunk over the past few years.

With this move, Gerard's strategy was that he could control her. She'd have no choice but to facilitate him as he ran roughshod over the company and its employees.

With her spending much more time in the corporate office, Powers volunteered to give up his own office to her, so he could work from home, which he preferred under his new scenario. The less time he spent in Gerard's presence, the better he liked it.

He was conflicted by the constant mixed signals Gerard used to keep him off balance. He also realized that he seriously misjudged Gerard from the beginning. But he couldn't wrap his arms around how he let that happen, or how he was going to deal with him.

55

Turning Lemons into Lemonade

Over the weekend, Powers got a call from his son, Todd in Charlotte, who wanted to share an experience he had at a hotel where he attended an engineering trade convention. Todd was a senior mechanical engineer with a specialty in liquid flow design. He led a team of engineers who designed breweries and chemical plants.

He had just returned from an engineering conference held at a hotel in Atlanta, that coincidentally had a HydroDyne installation. The hotel's maintenance engineer was there and had met Todd at one of the break-out sessions.

During the casual conversation, Todd mentioned that his father's company had developed this product that saved huge amounts of water in hotels and apartment buildings. The engineer responded, "Do you mean the HydroDyne? We have that system and we put it in a few years ago. When it was installed, the water reduction was huge, but now it's saving less and less water."

"Why do you think it's underperforming? Is there a way to adjust it to make it more efficient?"

"No idea. The system is too complicated and way above my pay grade."

Curious and concerned, Todd asked, "Can you show it to me? Maybe I can suggest how to improve its output."

"That would be great. I'll take you to see it at the end of the afternoon session."

When the conference ended, the two men went down to the basement to inspect the unit. Todd spent about twenty minutes checking out the system. He noticed a vibration coming from the backflow valve and traced it to a faulty gasket. He told the engineer that he would report the problem to his father.

The engineer shook hands and thanked him profusely.

When Todd finished telling his father the story, he offered his advice on correcting the situation. "Dad, that gasket is not the right spec. It must be made from a substantially stronger material. It's breaking down and the system will soon fail. You need to get on this right away."

Powers spent the weekend thinking about the issue, and on Monday morning, he called Gerard, who answered: "Why are you calling me?"

To soften Gerard's testy attitude a little, Powers responded, "Houston, we have a problem."

"What the fuck is that supposed to mean?"

"There's a flaw in the system, and they are about to fail."

"Are you fucking serious? How do you know that?"

"My son is an engineer and he checked out the unit in our Atlanta hotel installation. It's no longer reducing water consumption, and it's about to break down."

"Because your kid says so, we should drop everything and solve this mystery problem that doesn't exist. Why hasn't anyone else complained about this non-issue?"

"Atlanta was one of the first installations, and Johnson Park was onsite when it was installed and adjusted. We can expect that more of the older installations will hit similar problems."

Now Gerard was in a rage. "So, maybe that fucking Chink screwed up the installation. He didn't know what he was doing, anyway. That was obvious to me from the start."

"Gerard, don't blame this on Johnson. He holds two patents on the system and is responsible for its excellent performance. It's not about blame. It's about solving a problem that could bury us."

Gerard interrupted. Powers continued, "Will you just shut up and listen! I have a solution that will turn this disaster into a money-making opportunity."

Silence from Gerard, so he continued, "Following the introduction of the original system, which Atlanta has, we made several improvements and upgrades. We now create a tune-up package for every client whose installation took place before last year. We replace any necessary parts and return it to its original performance level."

"Big deal. So, where's the opportunity?"

"We charge $1,500 for the service. Our cost on the parts is under $100, and the labor is about $200. We can make better than a 500% profit on each service call. It becomes a new profit center."

"Okay, let me research it. I'm about to go to the East Coast, so I can't spend time on it now."

Thinking about Powers' idea, Gerard realized he could own it and look like a hero to the shareholders. And he could use this plan to pay himself a huge bonus.

56

New Prospect Categories

With Gerard and Emilio on the road more frequently, Powers stayed in the local area and made cold calls on properties throughout southwest Florida. One new prospect was a management firm that owned over 40 nursing homes all over Florida. They were very interested in receiving a proposal from HydroDyne. He was encouraged, as they were the size of some of Emilio's REIT clients.

Norman from Green Solutions was in Clearwater visiting a new client. He called Powers and suggested they meet for breakfast. At a small coffee shop near the beach, they discussed Norman's growing block of business.

"Dave, my sales are about to take off. One of my deacons owns a company that sells paper goods and cleaning supplies to hotels. He is now referring his customers to me, and we share the profits. This hotel up the street is one of those referrals."

"I was wondering why you had a client in Florida."

"Oh, I'll soon be all over the country. My deacon has a customer base in every state."

This gave Powers the idea to research companies similar to Green Solutions that were potential prospects for distributorships or referral partners.

He called utility audit companies with customer lists that were candidates for HydroDyne's system. Explaining the synergy from their client base, he quickly got three firms seriously interested. They all requested presentations to learn more.

The three audit companies were in Atlanta, Richmond and Hackensack, New Jersey, prompting him to set up video-conference calls with them. His enthusiasm, self-confidence and smooth delivery convinced each of them to join the HydroDyne distribution channel. He told them he would send out contracts right away.

Powers calculated the potential of this new category. The databases of just these three companies could produce well over $150 million in sales. If he only sold 10% of their prospects, he would earn three-quarters of a million dollars! And that's not counting the effect on the stock's share price. For the first time since founding the company, he felt it was about to turn the corner and skyrocket.

At the end of one of his most successful weeks, Powers wrote up reports on these, and all his new prospects into the Salesforce management system.

He took Elisa out to dinner that night to share his excitement over the week's activity.

"I'm afraid to share your enthusiasm over this news. We've come down so far. Just paying the bills every month depresses me."

"It's truly the beginning of a new era for HydroDyne. And it will end our stress. I promise, dear."

57

Ethical Lapse

One of the investors, Angelo Keyes was recommended by Newman to replace Powers on the board. Once appointed, he considered himself the advocate for the shareholders. In his self-assigned capacity, he questioned everything and was becoming an annoying participant. This raised an alarm with Gerard, who saw Keyes as potential interference with his plans for his long-term unimpeded dictatorship.

When Gerard returned from a trip to Orlando, bringing back several large orders, he told Newman he wanted to form an executive committee of the board, so the two of them could make changes with no interference from the new board member. She flatly refused, explaining that it would require a meeting of the entire board to pass such a resolution, and even then, it could be challenged in court.

Gerard responded, "We're lawyers and we know the laws, but none of the other shareholders are familiar with the statutes. Write the resolution, before Keyes comes on as a director. No one will know it exists, except us. And we can start voting ourselves salary increases and stock bonuses."

"We both could be disbarred for that. Not that it matters to you, since you no longer practice law. I can't afford to take that chance."

"Barbara, this is the compensation for the value we're delivering. The investors don't appreciate what we're accomplishing for them. And when they get their payout, they won't care how much we made."

"I'm still uncomfortable with this resolution."

"Look, I just signed you on to a generous deal, supplemented with stock bonuses that will make you rich when we sell the company. It will only take about two years."

This was a lot to digest, but it was an opportunity hard to pass up. She was seeing firsthand the recent sales growth and how fast the pace was accelerating.

She let the greed cloud her ethics. Thinking only about the vast potential at stake, she risked this one small transgression which would be almost impossible to uncover.

She wrote up the resolution and added it to the minutes of the previous board meeting. With that completed, Gerard instructed her to issue each of them 10,000 shares of stock.

58

Basic Sales 101

Powers emailed Emilio that he added over 50 new leads in the Salesforce database for him to follow up, including the large chain of nursing homes. He also had the three large referral partners onboard and awaiting contracts. He suggested to Emilio that they meet upon his return to the office to discuss implementing these deals. He ended by mentioning he got a large order from another hotel in Canada. He also copied Gerard.

Gerard responded before Emilio did, and told him that he would follow up on the referral prospects, and as soon as Emilio had time, he would make appointments to close the new leads. He also questioned the order from Canada and why was he still chasing leads from up there.

Powers replied he got a quote request, and they forwarded a purchase order. He asked, "Why would I turn down business anywhere in North America when the whole process is done through email?" He also suggested that they meet at the office to discuss the distributor prospects, as they all had huge potential and he didn't want to lose them through a misstep.

Gerard's response ignored his questions about turning down business outside the US, but he told Powers there was no need to meet to talk about the distributors, as the CEO, he knew how to handle them.

Gerard had a particular interest in the one distributor from Atlanta as they had an installation team on staff. Emilio's client had several apartment buildings in that area. He figured if he could sign them up, they could oversee the

163

installations for those buildings. He called and made an appointment to fly up to Atlanta the following week for a meeting.

Gerard then called the audit company in Richmond, the biggest of the three prospects, and spoke to the owner. After introducing himself, Gerard immediately dictated unreasonable terms and a 5% commission. The owner was taken aback and said, "I have no interest at this point in your new rules and terms. Dave Powers outlined an equitable program that gave us a split of the profit."

Gerard countered. "Our water-saving system is so good, that the customers will pay any amount we tell them. I can bump up the price and give you a bigger slice. So, don't give me that shit about not knowing how to come up with a fair and profitable formula. You're the one who doesn't know what the fuck he's talking about."

"Mr. Morbus, you don't understand Basic Sales 101. So, I don't think we have anything else to talk about. You have a good day."

When he heard the line disconnect, Gerard yelled into the mouthpiece, "Fuck you!"

And to the wall, "How dare that prick hang up on me? It was just as well, as I didn't want to have to educate a dumb fuck like him. And there is no way I'm going to let Powers end up getting commissions from a big client like that. I'll find another company with that kind of potential."

59

Added Casualties

Arriving at the offices of the new distributor in Atlanta, Gerard immediately sized up the situation. He decided that the two owners were Georgia yahoos who had a successful business but were not very sophisticated. The third person he met, who was their installation supervisor, was probably a good technician, but had no business acumen. His role was to manage a team of independent contractors who did all the installs.

The company's service offering included utility audits, plus repairs and installation of lighting, AC, and plumbing. Gerard spent a couple of hours with them, boasting about his vast history of successes, and learning about their operation without telling them much about HydroDyne. They concluded the meeting with an exchange of business cards, and Gerard promising to send them additional data on the system and the distributor agreement, all of which he had neglected to bring.

On the way back to Hartsfield airport, he thought about the supervisor Tommy Gage he had just met. Maybe he could use Gage to do the installs for the properties that Emilio's client had in the Atlanta area. Then, he wouldn't have to share the profit with the two owners.

He called Gage on his cell and asked him if he would be interested in coming to work for HydroDyne. He assured him he would make much more money and bonus shares of stock in a high-flying firm that was growing. They talked for a while, and Gage said he would think about it and get back to him the next day.

While waiting for his return flight to board, Gerard got a call from Newman. She phoned to tell him that she had just accepted the position of corporate counsel from her large insurance client. She advised him she would continue to serve on his board, but had to resign from her admin duties. He told her that he was pleased that she would stay on the board, and wished her luck in her new role.

He then called Amanda and asked her if she could meet him at Selva Grill downtown when he got back at about 6 that evening. He explained to her that some unexpected changes were about to occur that would benefit her. She had no plans for the evening and agreed to meet him at the popular downtown hotspot.

Gerard then called Salete and told her he wouldn't be back from Atlanta until late that night. Disappointed, she said she would make herself something for dinner and wait up for him unless it got too late.

On the return flight, he thought about this change in the dynamics at the office without Newman in the picture. He viewed this as a stroke of good luck, as he concluded that he could better control Amanda to do his surreptitious activity with the books. Newman had become defiant and more resistant to his requests to conduct activities that were seriously unethical or illegal. This, despite Gerard's threats of exposing her prior legal transgression.

Amanda got to the restaurant before Gerard and ordered a Cosmo. She was in her forties, divorced for over 20 years, and lived alone. She had long since given up on marriage after her break-up with an abusive husband who she had married while she was still in college. Her personality had a hard edge, and it reflected in her looks. She wore tight-fitting clothes that revealed a slightly overweight body with good curves. Her hair was brassy with dark roots, and her nails, perfume and makeup were all overdone.

Gerard arrived about 15 minutes later, kissed her on the cheek, and had a single malt scotch. He told Amanda about Newman's resignation, and offered her the position. She told him that in order for her to move to full time, she'd have to give up some of her bookkeeping customers that she handled on a freelance basis.

He assured her she would make much more working for him, so she accepted his offer. Over dinner, they had a few more drinks and then left. Gerard walked her back to the garage on Palm Avenue, where they were both parked. When they got to her car, he put his arms around her and kissed her passionately. She returned the kiss, pressing her crotch against him. When they broke, he said, "I promise that you will be delighted that you go full time with me. It is going to be an opportunity you won't regret."

When he got home, Salete was still awake. She greeted him with a kiss when he came in, and she could pick up the scent of a woman's fragrance.

60

Inconclusive Financials

While Gerard was in Atlanta, Angelo Keyes came into the office and introduced himself to Amanda. He asked to see a copy of the latest month's financial statements.

"I can't give you those without approval from Gerard."

"Yes, you can dear, I am now a member of the board, and one of the original investors. In fact, I was helping the firm with its launch, even before Dave Powers joined the team. I'm the one who brought him in."

"I apologize. I didn't realize your position in the company." She printed down the statements.

Keyes brought them into the conference room and began reviewing them. When he finished, he came back to her with a few questions about a certain posting, which she answered. Angelo wrote a few notes on the paperwork and put the reports in his briefcase. He then browsed around in the file cabinets. Every so often, he would pull out a file and look through it.

Seeing what he was doing, she chided, "Make sure you return every file exactly where you found it. It took me weeks to straighten out the filing, and I'm not about to do it again."

Keyes left, telling her he would see her again shortly.

When Gerard phoned in, Amanda told him about Keyes' visit. Although annoyed, he recognized that as a director, he had every right to inspect the books. And besides, Gerard didn't want Keyes to think he had anything to hide. But he also knew he had to make a few changes to their file system. He told Amanda that when he got back, they would review the files with her and move certain sensitive paperwork to a locked file cabinet in his office.

When Keyes left, he met three of the other shareholders for lunch at Casey Key Fish House. The open-air restaurant sat on the Intracoastal Waterway in Nokomis. Its boat docks made it a favorite gathering hole for fishermen and pleasure boaters.

The three were former partners at a trash hauling company in Detroit. They were tough Italians who grew up in a neighborhood run by mobsters. They all invested in the company at Keyes' recommendation and were anxious to know how their money was doing.

Keyes shared some numbers from the report showing rapidly escalating sales that could surpass $4 million by year-end. Tommy Cantarella, the largest shareholder, was enthused. "Now we're getting somewhere. Dave was right. This guy will salvage the company."

Keyes answered, "It does look like they solved the sales problem, but the costs are going through the roof. The new bookkeeper doesn't have the books up-to-date, so I can't tell if we're profitable. But we're in the right direction."

61

A Hard Day at the Office

After Gerard spent the entire Monday morning on the phone, there were only three calls of any consequence. The first was from the CEO of the Atlanta distributor. His angry call was not what Gerard wanted at the start of his day.

Shouting into the phone, he said, "Morbus, you're a cesspool bottom feeder. Tommy Gage told us about your job offer. He said he could never work for a slimy creep like you. And we don't want anything to do with you either. How can you even sleep at night?"

Gerard's response was typical when someone disagreed with him: "Go fuck yourself. You and your shit-shoveling country clowns will be broke before the end of the year. And I sleep just fine."

The second call came in right after the first and did nothing to improve his black mood. His tenant, who rented a nearby furnished condo from him, moved out over the weekend. She was two months behind and couldn't pay the rent. Although he was polite, it took all he had to avoid telling her in his colorful language what he really thought.

The third call was from Powers' new distributor in north Jersey. He and his partner wanted to schedule installation and sales training at HydroDyne's offices. Gerard set a date with them to visit in two weeks. During the discussion, he came up with another idea. "I have a two bed, two bath furnished condo near the office that you're welcome to use. It will save you a few days of hotel costs."

They accepted his generous offer and thanked him.

Following that call, Gerard went out to the front office and said to Amanda, "I want you to look at a condo I own. I just offered it to the guys from New Jersey when they come for training, but it needs to be cleaned up. Then, I'll buy you lunch."

The condo was a wreck. Dishes were piled in the sink, linens were scattered on the floor, and the entire place hadn't been cleaned in months. A couple of pieces of furniture had been damaged, and some wall hangings were missing.

Gerard exploded. "That fucking bitch! I gave her a discount on the rent, and what does she do? She trashes the place and steals my stuff."

Amanda wrinkled her nose. "It smells awful."

"Hire a cleaning service to clean the entire condo, including the dishes and laundry. I'll have Salete replace a few items. Also, stock the place with some non-perishable food and get some wine and liquor."

They went to Gecko's for a quick lunch and he told her he had big plans for her. He expected her to follow his exact orders without reservation, even if she thought they were questionable. And if she did this, her rewards would be substantial.

Leaving the restaurant, he handed her the key to the condo. "Get a few more keys made and keep one for yourself."

Amanda felt very excited about her future. As a single woman, she made a comfortable living, but there was always the insecurity of the future, when she couldn't work. Gerard could pay her generously, and this opportunity could ensure her financial security. And further, she found his brash style attractive.

When they got back to the office, Gerard called Salete and told her about the condition at the condo. The company would arrange for the cleanup, but he wanted her to see what furniture and accessories needed to be replaced.

Troubled by the news, she said, "Why we keep it? Sell it and be done with a headache."

He also shared his idea about the distributors using it, so the company could reimburse them for all the replacement items. That pleased her. She asked, "Will company clean up, too?"

He said, "Yes. As long as we are using it for out-of-town visits from our distributors and customers, I'll have HydroDyne pay the rent and the maintenance."

Later that day, Keyes came into the office and made some small talk with Gerard. He then said he wanted to look at some other reports. With Gerard's approval, he went to Amanda and asked for the sales reports for the previous six months.

Angelo took the paperwork into the conference room and spent the next hour reviewing it. He was impressed with the new orders that had come in from a growing list of clients.

After he packed the reports in his briefcase, he walked back to Gerard's office and complimented him on how well Emilio was doing with his sales effort.

Gerard corrected him. "It's not just Emilio who's responsible for the sales. I've got the closing skills. Emilio contacts his Spick friends in Miami, and I wrap up the deals. He just landed a huge deal, and I'll close it tomorrow. It's dozens of buildings on a Savings-Share plan."

Keyes then asked, "What about profitability? The books are incomplete, so I can't tell if we're making money."

"Oh, we're making money, alright. I'm timing the posting so we don't show too much profit until the next quarter. We'll have more cash for taxes, then. Trust me, our margins are huge."

Relieved by the explanation, Keyes left. "Sounds great. I'll see you next week."

When he left, Gerard realized he couldn't have Keyes walk into the office and snoop around any time he chose. After thinking about it for a while, Gerard came up with a solution to get him out of the way.

62

Too Good a Deal?

Gerard called Keyes the following week and asked him to come in to discuss a business deal. When Keyes arrived, he could see that Gerard was excited, and couldn't wait to hear the news.

"Angelo, we closed the deal I mentioned. It's our biggest Savings-Share plan, by far. It will be worth millions. My problem is the financing. We don't have the funds for a deal this big."

"Gerard, if the deal is solid, financing is no problem."

"Great, here's what I have in mind. I know you're connected to some investment banking guy and if you want to start up a small finance operation, you can easily make six figures."

"Sure, I'm interested. Give me more details."

Gerard then walked him through the process where the customer would get all his buildings installed for $2 million, with no money upfront. Once installed, the water savings cover the costs in six months. HydroDyne takes all the savings for three years.

"Angelo, after HydroDyne gets paid in full, we split the savings for the balance of the three years. So, you'll clear over $1.5 million, less the cost of the funds. Are you in?"

"For that kind of easy money? You bet your ass I'm in."

"One caveat. If you take this deal, you have to resign from the board. You can't hold a board seat while you're making a profit from the company. You okay with that?"

"If it's a one-time deal, I'll pass. But if you can sell more financed deals, then we're good to go."

"I'm confident we can sell one a month, and later even increase that number."

"One a month? I can get rich on the financing alone!"

63

Letdown and Uplift

When the partners from the New Jersey distributor flew to Sarasota for training with Gerard, Powers joined them. The first period included everything required for making sales calls and presenting the system to prospective clients. Gerard spent most of the time telling anecdotes about his sales successes and sexual conquests, plus a few off-color jokes.

He provided very little detail identifying prospects, explaining the technology, or closing the sale. Instead of an all-day agenda, he ended by noon.

After the lunch break, Gerard ran the critical installation class. This training was normally conducted by the engineer, Johnson Park, but since he resigned, Gerard had not replaced him. Instead, Gerard did a cursory and clumsy job of describing the installation. When he couldn't answer most of their questions, he offered to send his best installer to direct the onsite installation of their first order.

Since they expected a two-day session, Gerard suggested Powers take them to play golf the next day. Powers was relieved at their enthusiastic response. It eased his embarrassment of the woefully inadequate training.

When the two executives returned to New Jersey, Gerard told Amanda to have the condo cleaned again.

The next day, he suggested they stop by the condo after work to see Salete's décor changes and how well it was cleaned. He told her they would go to dinner later.

When they got there, they were both impressed with Salete's work. Amanda commented, "Wow. This condo is beautiful. Anyone would love to live here."

Gerard opened a bottle of cabernet. Taking a sip, he said, "You picked this? It's good."

They sat on the sofa talking about the day's activities. Amanda wore a straight short skirt that rode half way up her muscled, tanned thighs, revealing her best feature. Gerard leaned over and put his hand between them. She let out a whimper. He pulled her to him, kissing her hard as he fondled her moist crotch. They moved to the bedroom where he hungrily watched her undress. She had the firm body of a workout enthusiast. Her torso was a little heavier than he liked, but her legs were perfect.

Gerard pulled off his pants, climbed on top of her and quickly climaxed. And as usual, he rushed into the bathroom to clean himself off and then returned to the bed.

After resting a few minutes, he went back to the living room for the wine. He was still wearing his socks, but she opted not to question it. They sat in bed, finishing the wine before they resumed their lovemaking, this time at a more relaxed pace.

Spent from the sex, they showered together a bit awkwardly and left the condo. He asked if she would like to stop for dinner, but she declined. Gerard brought her back to the office, where she picked up her car and drove home.

Lying in bed in her bland apartment, she thought about the night's implications. Amanda was attracted to Gerard, but reluctant to cross the line with her boss. When he came on to her, she succumbed. She had no idea where this tryst was going, yet she wanted to ride it out. She was unfulfilled with her solitary lifestyle and yearned for a change. However, her terrible marriage had kept her from putting herself out there.

Amanda knew an affair with a married man was the worst scenario, yet found his rough, crude demeanor to be exhilarating and sexy. And he was already giving her things she couldn't afford. She envisioned living in his condo, but it was a long shot. She fell asleep enjoying the blissful remnants of the evening and inhaling his muskiness.

64

Filling the Bone Yard

At lunchtime the next day, Gerard went to the mall and walked into Saks Fifth Avenue. He wandered around until he found the handbag section. Seeing his confusion, a matronly clerk in an expensive suit asked if she could help.

"I need a handbag for a special person. I want to impress her. Price is no concern."

Smiling, she said, "I think I know exactly what you're looking for."

She took him around to the other side of the counter and withdrew a Prada bag out of the display case. As she handed it to him, she said, "Any woman would fall in love with this magnificent creation."

Gerard palmed his company credit card, without seeing the $4,300 price tag, and saying, "Perfect. I'll take it. Wrap it up."

Back at the office, he handed Amanda the Saks shopping bag. Amanda excitedly opened it and shrieked. He hadn't removed the price tag, and as she saw what it cost, tears tracked down her cheeks. She kissed him, squeezed her breasts against him and thanked him.

Later, Gerard called Newman.

"Barbara, it's Gerard. I need you to stop by after work and sign the minutes of today's executive session of the board meeting."

"What's it all about? I know nothing about any meeting."

"Of course, you don't. I held it today to change a few clauses in my contract, and to distribute some shares of stock from the employee pool."

"Look, Gerard. I can't do this anymore. This is far too dangerous. I have too much at stake. Stop this before you get us into serious legal trouble."

"Barbie, doll. You said it. You have too much at stake. Are you forgetting that I hold your law license in my hands?"

"Are you threatening me?"

"What would happen if I filed a complaint with the Florida Bar? Now, come here and sign these damn minutes."

Later, she reviewed the pages that Amanda had typed and signed them. Then she turned to Gerard and said, "Let me be crystal clear. This is the last document I ever sign for you."

"You'll come in whenever I need your signature. It's not negotiable."

"No. It's over. After your call, I sent an affidavit to my own attorney outlining your blackmail tactics. I hereby resign from the board. Now. If you try to bring me down, you are coming with me. I have documented everything."

Gerard uncharacteristically held his anger in check. "You have made a huge mistake to think you can cross me. Try to use what you have against me and I will tear you to shreds. Now get the fuck out of my office."

After she left, Gerard called Amanda and told her to edit the board minutes document Newman had just signed. He had her rewrite the middle page that awarded 500 shares of stock to both Newman and him, changing Newman's name to Amanda's. She brought the edited document back for him to proofread. He approved it and told her, "You have now officially become a shareholder."

She bent down as he sat in his chair, hugged him and planted a wet, tongue-filled kiss on his mouth. He reached his arm around her and fondled her right breast. Rising, she said, "Wait here." She scampered to the reception area, locked the front door and put out the lights. The only illumination came from Gerard's laptop.

Amanda knelt in front of him, unzipped his pants and sucked his penis, which was quickly hardening. When he came in a minute, she got up, went to the bathroom nude and washed her face. She walked back to his office in the gloomy light, and sat on his couch. Spreading her legs, she said, "Now it's my turn."

65

The Day from Hell

Powers found an unexpected email in his inbox from his Atlanta client, telling him they resigned from HydroDyne after their disastrous meeting with Gerard Morbus. Not knowing anything, he called and learned precisely what went down. He was shocked Gerard would commit such an unethical act, particularly with a new client. He had to confront him on it.

Around the same time, Gerard got a text from the new distributor in New Jersey, with a copy to Powers.

Good news! We just got a test order from a property in the Bronx with 30,000 apartments. Schedule an installer to oversee the project, as agreed. The order is for $2,000, and with the results documented, we do the entire series of buildings.

Gerard wrote back.

There's no way I'm sending an engineer to New York, to risk his life in that dangerous, gang-ridden part of the city, and pay expenses for a shitty test order. Get the entire property, and you'll get as much help as you need.

Minutes later Powers jumped into the fray.

Gerard, this order has huge potential, probably more than any other customer we have. It's for Co-Op City and it is very safe. You promised to send someone up there if they got an order. And despite the size, it's a serious customer.

The distributor responded.

Gerard, you can't go back on your word. We flew down there to Sarasota for training, which was an embarrassment

181

at best, and now you renege on your promise? What kind of bullshit is that?

Ten minutes later, Gerard wrote back.

I just checked and found out New York City has very strict building codes. There is no way I'm going to risk my company's reputation fighting with inspectors in that bribe-infested cesspool. So, New York is off-limits. Find customers somewhere else.

The distributor answered.

You specifically told us, and it's in the manual. There are no territories. We can sell anywhere we have a customer. So, stop this smokescreen and send someone up here right away. We don't want to jeopardize this prime client.

Gerard fired back.

Look assholes, you don't tell me what to do. I run this operation, and the distributors take orders from me, not the other way around. If you're not mature enough to follow orders, then I don't need your fucking business. So, send back the manual. You are no longer a distributor.

Appalled, Powers wrote back.

Gerard, what the hell is the matter with you? You don't ever treat anyone with that kind of contempt. You mention "mature" in your text. But your response was anything but. Act like the CEO we thought we hired, not some uneducated buffoon.

Gerard phoned Powers, blasting him, "Dave, don't you ever, ever talk to me or write to me with that kind of disrespect again, particularly when a customer is in the loop. Who the fuck do you think you are? If you ever pull a fucked-up stunt like that again, I will bury you. Are we clear?"

"You're right. I should have talked to you offline. It doesn't forgive your actions. You just fired a distributor with huge potential."

"No, they were a couple of jerks, like the yahoos in Atlanta. But you're not savvy enough to pick the winners."

"You're the one who's being a jerk. You just blew two new distributors. I'm going to meet with our investors about your behavior. Now, you get *your* shit together. You are expendable."

Gerard was furious, first with the distributor, then Powers' text, and his affront on the phone. No one got away with this insolence or threats. He vowed Powers would never receive his scheduled stock bonus, or see a penny in commission. Ever. Gerard also decided to reject his expenses. He was history.

66

Last Man Standing

After Powers got the call from the distributor confirming they were canceling their contract, he called Newman. "Yesterday, I had an abusive text and phone call exchange with Gerard and a new dealer. Is he having some kind of stress meltdown?"

"I've experienced some personal issues with Gerard. I resigned from the board. However, that's related to an offer from my largest client. But there were other issues I'm not at liberty to share. Maybe you should get back on the board, as there's a vacancy now."

The conversation took him by surprise, and he called Keyes to ask him about the situation. "Angelo, what's going on with the board, since Barbara Newman has resigned?"

"I don't know what you're talking about. I haven't heard a word about her quitting."

"Well, it doesn't end there. After my new distributor opened a 30,000-apartment account, he insulted them, reneged on their deal, and fired them."

"That doesn't make sense. Why? What caused it?"

"No idea. They have enormous potential. As a board member, you need to get to him and find out what's going on."

"First you should know I also resigned. I'm now involved in a Savings-Share deal to finance installations. I can't wear both hats."

"Good for you, but what about the board?"

"Because of that, I'm more involved than ever with HydroDyne. I'll call Gerard and ask about Barbara. I'll let you know."

Powers was worried. He always felt comfortable that Newman had his back and watched out for the best interests of the company. She was gone, and his safety-valve director Keyes left the board and was doing a side business deal with Gerard.

Now, there was no one to keep Gerard's questionable decisions and angry outbursts under control. No guard rails. Even more devastating to his financial relief was the loss of three important new clients. The expected income potential was quickly dissipating, and his fear about the failure of the company grew exponentially.

Gerard had successfully marginalized him, and he was using the same tactics on the others. He was the only one left on the board. This was a disaster. He must find a way to save his company.

67

The Gifted Salesman

Salete and Gerard enjoyed dinner at his favorite restaurant, a bistro in the Rosemary District near downtown Sarasota. Owner Jon Mills greeted them. He also owned the apartment building on the same property. Gerard smoothly asked him when he was planning to order the HydroDyne system for his building. Mills told him that their cash flow was tight, but he was still interested. Gerard explained he could install the system with no upfront payment with the new Savings-Share plan. It appealed to Mills and he said he would call him the next day to arrange a demonstration for his maintenance manager.

Gerard turned to his wife, who was bored and staring at her drink. He boasted, "I'm such a gifted salesman. I could sell shit to a sewer treatment plant. And with my skill, Emilio is making a fortune in commission on accounts I closed. Maybe he can speak to those guys in Spanish, but then I have to do the hard sell and close the deal with the white guys in the front office."

"Geraldo, do not overlook strength of relationship. Emilio has powerful bond with other Cubans. They protect and help each other."

"Salete, that's bullshit. The Cuban hombre thing just gets him in the door. It's my talent making the difference. I'm going on the road by myself next week, and watch what I bring in."

Before leaving the next day, he told Amanda he'd like to get together with her when he got back. He also had her order a case of wine delivered to the condo, and to keep four bottles for herself.

Gerard began his road trip with firm appointments in St. Augustine and Jacksonville. Both were a waste of time, as neither property manager was convinced of the value of the system. He spent the next several days making cold calls, ending in Tallahassee. Despite his persistence, he couldn't meet with anyone except a maintenance supervisor at a mid-rise apartment building in Gainesville. It was his last stop on the way back to Sarasota. And the manager expressed no interest.

It did not stop Gerard. He needed to make a sale before returning from his trip, and he was determined to close. He repeated his entire sales pitch, telling the manager the huge savings would get him a promotion. The prospect merely smiled and said that there was no way a reduction in water cost would get him to the next level in his company. He ended the meeting.

Exasperated by not making that sale, or any other on this trip, Gerard vented his frustration. He berated the manager. "Just so you know, everyone buys my system. You're probably the stupidest Spick I ever called on. I bet you get fired for not buying it."

The furious manager ordered him to leave.

Driving down I-75, he called Amanda, hoping the sound of her voice would cheer him up. He told her to meet him at the condo at 7, and to order takeout. His return was a day earlier than Salete expected him home. He also told her to call Speedy Petey, a car detailer, and schedule him to come to the office to clean and wax his Mercedes the next day.

They quietly shared dinner and a bottle of wine, followed by a trip to the bedroom for what Amanda anticipated to be a night of great sex. Unfortunately, Gerard was exhausted and frustrated by his sales failure to make even one sale. Their only round of intercourse, with his half-hearted effort, ended with him falling asleep after he had a quick orgasm, and her unfulfilled.

Gerard awoke at 5, showered and drove to the office. Amanda got up at 6:30, went home to change and came in about 9.

About an hour later, Salete happened to drive by the office and saw Gerard's car parked in his usual spot by the back door. And she realized that he must have been back in town the night before. This bolstered her suspicions about his escapades. She loathed infidelity, despite its old-school acceptance in Brazil.

68

Some New Blood

Gerard sat in a funk as he shuffled papers on his teak desk. The previous evening's unfulfilling tryst with Amanda capped a week of total disappointment. He rationalized that his bad luck of having to pitch no one but imbeciles all week caused his failure in bed.

He broke out of his reverie when Jon Mills called and said he wanted to come to the office to discuss the installation at his apartment building.

When Mills arrived, Gerard greeted him with smiles and back slaps. He walked him around, and then brought him into his office. Mills was anxious to hear about the Savings-Share program.

When Gerard outlined the basic concept, Mills recognized the financing was expensive, but it enabled him to grow more efficient immediately. He didn't hesitate to book the installation.

As they sat around after Mills signed the contract, Gerard thought of an idea that would help him with the company's management. "Jon, would you consider joining the firm's board of directors?"

Intrigued, he raised a few questions. "Not to sound mercenary, but does the position pay a stipend?"

"No. It's not a paid position, but we directors are issued periodic stock bonuses. And that can be very lucrative."

"With the company's pace of growth, that could be an attractive incentive. I think I would like to join your company."

"You may also be interested in investing in the company, as we are still accepting funds. And I can tell you, the stock is about to take off like a rocket."

"Sounds intriguing. Let me see if I can move some funding."

"Dig deep. The timing is perfect."

"Forward a copy of your financials to me, and any pro forma documents that are available. I'll get back to you shortly."

After Mills left, Gerard had Amanda change the documents to have Mills fulfill the remainder of Newman's term on the board. He also directed her to prepare certain financial documents to be sent to him.

Could this turn of events have worked out any better for him?

69

The Squeeze Play

Powers was having difficulty getting a few key investors together to confront Gerard. The company was sinking. He needed to address that situation quickly, but none saw any issues rising to the level of questioning Gerard's decisions.

In the meantime, he emailed Gerard inquiring about his commissions and expenses. He also asked for an update on the scores of leads he had been posting to the Salesforce database. There was no activity shown in the reports.

A few days later, Gerard responded, explaining that there were no commissions due, as the company only paid on new business, and not on existing prospects. His expenses were rejected as they had not been approved in advance.

Infuriated, Powers tried to call Gerard, but his call went to voicemail. He emailed back, attaching his detailed note he had authored at his meeting with Gerard, setting parameters for his compensation. It all conflicted with Gerard's response.

When Powers again asked about his leads, Gerard responded that Emilio was too busy with *real* customers, and didn't have time for Powers' weak prospects.

Powers answered that he would close the orders on his leads.

Gerard fired back: "You are not trained in the latest product features and terms, so you're not authorized to close any orders."

Powers then drove to the office, barged past the front desk, and directly into Gerard's office.

Gerard jumped up and shouted, "You can't come in here without an appointment. I have no time to talk to you."

"What the hell are you blabbering about? I hired you, so don't tell me what I can do."

"And you made me the CEO with total control. Now get the fuck out of here!"

That triggered a shouting match to nowhere. Frustrated, Powers went home. After he calmed down, he asked Angelo Keyes to meet him for coffee the following week.

That night Powers took Elisa out for their usual Friday night date. They drove down to Cassariano's in Venice. On the way, he shared the details of his verbal slugfest with Gerard. "His anger is influencing his decisions and driving away our customers. I'm convinced he is trying to get me to resign."

"You're both alpha personalities who constantly bang heads. You made him the CEO, so despite your urge to lead, you must back off."

"Believe me, I try. But his rage is costing us clients and money."

"Then you have to get help from the other shareholders and rein him in."

"Once again, you read my mind. I'm meeting with Angelo Keyes next week. If together we can't get Gerard in line, the company will fail. I'm really scared."

70

From Bad to Worse

At 8:30 the following Friday, Powers walked into First Watch, a local breakfast chain on Main Street, where Keyes was sitting in a booth with Tommy Cantarella. Dave was pleased that Cantarella joined the meeting as he was the leader of his small group of investors. Dave was concerned, however, as neither of them looked like they wanted to be there.

Keyes led off the discussion. "Okay, Dave, we're here. Now, what's so damn important?"

Powers took them through his role following Gerard's engagement, and how he was systematically marginalized. They listened intently, but heard no serious threat to the health of the company. Then Powers described how Gerard stymied his sales and destroyed the relationship with three distributors.

Cantarella said, "This doesn't make sense. I find it hard to believe."

Powers documented all the details and had them read Gerard's text message exchange with the New Jersey CEO.

Keyes said, "Why would Gerard deliberately sabotage sales? It affects *his* long-term income. I'll ask."

Cantarella added, "Dave, I have the highest respect for you. If it weren't for you, the company would have failed a long time ago. I agree with Angelo. None of this makes sense, but we'll follow up, for sure."

At the end of the week, Keyes called Powers, "I met with Gerard and asked him to explain your complaints. He was pissed that you came to us, but he answered every charge you made with credible justifications."

"Of course, he's going to cover his tracks. He's full of shit."

"He also told us that sales and profits were growing beyond projection. He thought we could flip the company in the next two years."

"That doesn't justify what he's done."

"Dave, given his responses and the good news about the future, our advice is to sit back and wait for your payout. In the big picture, these are small claims compared to what you'll get when we sell the company."

"Keep in mind Gerard is a smooth talker. If he's sabotaging my sales efforts, he has another agenda that none of us know about. Keep careful tabs on him. He'll screw all of us."

After hanging up, Powers knew that Gerard now had even more reason to deny him his compensation. He'd be wasting his time soliciting business for the company. His only comfort was that two of the shareholders were now paying closer attention to Gerard's actions.

Gerard, however, saw it differently. *How did they dare question my authority and my decisions? These ungrateful pricks have no appreciation of what I'm doing for them and they were ready to lynch me. I gave them the chance to make a fortune for themselves.*

Well, I'm done with those thankless bastards. I'm going to take my sweet revenge out on the shareholders and burn them all.

He wrote an email memo to the investors.

To all Shareholders,

Turning this company from a failure to a profitable entity has been a far more difficult task than any of you, or I for that matter, have expected. Every day, I face a problem, some of epic proportions, that I must solve. Recently, I was confronted with a situation that without my immediate intercession would have destroyed the company.

194

I learned that there is a flaw in the design of the original system, most likely the fault of our former engineer, Johnson Park. He specified the wrong material for a part, and it was causing the system to malfunction.

The cost of replacing that part in every system sold is staggering. But I came up with a solution. Instead of considering it a warranty problem, I'm offering our clients an upgrade and tune-up of their system for a nominal cost of $1,500. The service would include a stipulation that the improved system performance of the system, would save them the upgrade cost in less than one year. Not one client has turned down the offer.

This is the thinking necessary to turn around a firm that is plagued with endless problems. Fortunately, the adults are in charge!

Gerard Morbus, Chairman and CEO

When Powers got home that afternoon, he was dumbfounded by the outrageous email. How could Gerard so shamelessly take credit for the solution he had provided him?

He then went to the Salesforce site to post his two recent leads he got, although he felt doing so was a waste of time. When he logged in, he was shocked to find no leads listed there. His entire listing file was blank. He searched for some of the names he had previously posted, thinking they were misfiled. Every search came up empty. His two years of effort showed no activity from him at all. He sat there stunned. Gerard had isolated him.

He told Elisa about his call with Keyes. "Unfortunately, it went exactly as I expected. Gerard justified his every move. And the weak shareholders did not challenge him. All they accomplished was making Gerard angrier and warning him to be more cautious. But there's more." Dave then told her about the Salesforce deletions of his prospects and clients.

"How could he get away with what he's doing to you? Are you going to get any of the pay that he promised you for all your work?"

"Bottom line for us is that there will be no commissions, expenses, or stock bonuses. Zero income from HydroDyne until the company is sold."

"What happens if the company fails, or he causes it to implode? I'm getting a very bad feeling about this guy. I don't trust him."

"Elisa, I have the same feeling. The shareholders are being manipulated. If the company fails, we are wiped out. We just won't be able to live on the small amount of retirement funds we have left."

He took Elisa in his arms as the emotion caused by their conversation overwhelmed them both. He rocked her back and forth and the sobs turned into a flood of tears.

71

A New Tenant

Gerard and Salete were back at the restaurant in the Rosemary District having dinner when Jon Mills greeted them. Gerard asked him how the new system was working out. He said that the feedback from the property manager was excellent.

He mentioned he was renovating his house on Lido Key and was looking for a furnished rental for about six months. He asked if any of Gerard's apartment clients had a unit available.

Gerard said he owned a condo he could rent out on a month-to-month basis. The restauranteur, aware of Gerard's sense of taste, said he would take it sight unseen. He was desperate for a place to live and he did not want to go to a hotel. Salete was quietly relieved, as she suspected that Gerard was using the apartment for his dalliances.

The next morning Gerard came into the office ecstatic about his new scheme. He gave some paperwork to Amanda and told her to make the mortgage payments on his condo from the company account. One customer needed a short-term rental, so he offered the condo as a perk for purchasing the system. He omitted the fact that the customer was actually paying Gerard rent.

Gerard also gave her a long-term lease agreement that he wrote up for the company's ongoing usage.

Amanda handled it, but was disappointed, as she had hoped that he would let her move in. However, she remained optimistic, thinking if their relationship continued to grow, maybe after this rental term ended, he'd offer her the place. When the time came, she was sure she could convince him.

72

Mixing Work and Pleasure

With profits growing as sales continued to spiral up, Gerard looked for ways to pad his income. He granted himself a raise by creating an executive session of the board and forging the minutes.

Unsatisfied, he saw an opportunity to transform his expense account into an income source. He paid all his expenses, legitimate or otherwise, with his corporate credit card, and he also put in for the same charges on an expense voucher. This way, the company would pay his credit card bills, plus write him checks, paying twice for each expense.

Feeling the euphoria of the added income only fueled his greed. He then paid for every personal purchase he made with the company card, followed by vouchers with the same charges. Gerard bought cases of expensive wine and scotch to be shipped to his house, ordered custom suits and monogrammed shirts, plus his lunches and dinners, new luggage for traveling, and everything but his groceries, all paid through his credit card and again with his vouchers.

He traded in the Mercedes and leased an Aston Martin, telling Amanda to have the lease payments processed through the company.

Despite the previous failures in his selling forays, Gerard made trips to pitch business. These trips proved to be no more productive than his earlier attempts, yet were more frequent, and to more exotic places. Gerard would book a premium hotel suite at luxury tourist destinations like New Orleans and Chicago, enjoying a mini-vacation while making a pitch for the hotel's account.

Occasionally, he brought Amanda along. Their first excursion together was to San Diego, and they stayed at the Grand Del Mar Resort. For a few days, they lounged on deck chairs at the pool, enjoying the Pacific, the sunshine, and mild weather. Gerard would order tropical drinks and snacks during the late morning, and after 12, they'd head up to their suite, where they would get into bed and enjoy a *nooner*. After the sex, they went back down to the pool for lunch. The odd couple spent the rest of the day on the lounge chairs and sipped drinks.

The other guests couldn't help but notice the huge age difference and how the couple seemed sexually attracted to each other. They quickly became the gossip story of the hotel, as it was obvious that the older gentleman had brought his attractive *niece* on vacation.

On the fourth afternoon, wearing a swim suit, and flip-flops, Gerard made a half-hearted sales pitch to the hotel. Since he was a guest, the manager humored him, but there was no interest in the system.

By the fifth day, after two lovemaking sessions during the day and night, Gerard was spent, while Amanda was just getting warmed up.

She suggested, "Why don't you get some Viagra, so we can spend more time making love?"

"A great idea, Amanda honey, I'll make a discreet inquiry at the concierge desk. If anyone can score some meds, it will be them."

And sure enough, Gerard got the wonder drug and performed like a young stud.

"Wow! That was a much harder erection. You also lasted so much longer. And you didn't have an erection lasting more than four hours. Hahaha."

The following day, despite Gerard's Johnson snapping to attention every time she snapped her fingers, his soft flaccid body was on the verge of becoming a blob of blubber on the bed. Amanda then flew back to the office, and Gerard went on to Phoenix, and finally back to Sarasota.

Whenever he could, he timed his travel to arrive at the office late in the day, and after hours enjoy some oral sex on his couch with Amanda before he returned home. Following this trip, he went straight home to rest his wasted body. He had nothing left for Salete.

Gerard was now gone more frequently, making trips nearly every week. And returning home late at night, he almost always carried the scent of a woman on him. Salete was certainly not fooled by his lame excuses of jetlag, and she was incensed at what was happening as their marriage grew lifeless.

73

Where's the Evidence?

After Gerard told her about the company paying the condo mortgage, Salete saw their checking account balance was climbing rapidly. She asked, "Geraldo, how is there much more money in bank? Is more than your monthly fee. Are you again doing something not legal?"

"Don't worry your pretty little head. My fees are increasing. And I'm getting bonuses because the company is doing so well."

She worried about the deliveries coming to the house. "And Geraldo, who is sending gifts and liquor and so much expensive wines to us? This never happens before. I see all new suits and shirts from tailor. Your clothes become more than mine."

He grew irritated. "Why are you questioning my success? The shareholders pay for all this, because I make them money. So be happy and don't ask me any more about it."

With his evasive answers and irrational response, she became convinced Gerard was siphoning off money from the company. And she knew that sooner or later he would get caught.

She called her brother. "Diego, something is wrong with Geraldo. He takes money from company, much money. And many boxes come to the house every week with wine and gifts. I ask him and he lies to me. He makes lines on his forehead and not look in my eyes when it not the truth. But I know. It will be bad."

Diego agreed that something illegal was being foisted. "I'll be in Miami in a few weeks, and I'll meet you in Sarasota."

While Salete revealed the illicit income increases, she did not share her suspicions about Gerard's infidelity. She would wait to see if she could gather more evidence before she acted on that liaison.

She'd track his travel and check his time at the office. Salete knew that most days Amanda was the only employee there. The install teams worked from remote locations, and Emilio spent nearly all of his time on the East Coast, traveling from the Keys to Palm Beach.

She knew this would not end well.

74

Success Has Its Privileges

Thanks to Emilio's Herculean sales effort, the orders climbed in numbers and size. And the installation teams had become so efficient that profits grew.

Gerard sent an interim report to the shareholders, boasting about the company's success. He focused on sales, touting their unprecedented increases.

Since profits were dropping, due to his unearned income, double-dipping, and his generosity to Amanda, his report glossed over the shrinking margins. He ignored any explanation of the reduced percentages.

Of course, he took most of the credit for the sales spike, despite his dismal performance. He used phrases like: *My management of the sales process; As a result of my personal involvement; My closing skills.* This gave him all the credit for the success of the effort. And he was certain this smokescreen would keep anyone from asking why the profit percentage had dropped so substantially recently.

He believed his propaganda, convinced he was a terrific salesman. He could still close the prospects who turned him down. It led him to plan another series of trips to call on these same properties. Only this time, he found a better way to fly.

When he first started traveling for the company, he flew only coach, then business class, and finally first class. Then he heard about shared flights on private jets.

This was the ultimate choice for someone at his success level. And while the ads claimed it was economical, the cost was substantially more than first class. The planes were luxuriously appointed, catering to sophisticated flyers who expected the finest amenities. And the plush cabins were staffed by the most beautiful flight attendants in the air.

This level of travel was in a league by itself. Gerard justified it by assuming it had the potential for encounters with new prospects for the company.

75

Haunted by the Past

As Gerard was jetting around, two men arrived at the office who would rattle Amanda, then Gerard. They were tall, dressed in navy blue business suits and ties. Amanda was alone and surprised, as visitors rarely came to the office unannounced. They produced FBI identification from the Miami office. Shocked, she asked, "Why are you here?"

The shorter man produced a photo of a man with a full beard, long frizzy hair, and dark, horn-rimmed glasses. "Do you recognize this man? Does he work here? His name is Harold Payne, but he may use an assumed name."

Intimidated by the two imposing men and their FBI credentials, she looked at the photo and haltingly answered, "I have no idea who that is. I'm sure I have never seen him. Why are you looking for him?"

Ignoring her question, he asked again, "Are you sure this isn't someone you know or have seen?"

They then asked if anyone else in the office could look at the photo. When she explained she was alone, and seldom had visitors, they thanked her, gave her their cards and left.

The intrusion stunned Amanda. She was not easily intimidated, but these two agents got to her. And the photo creeped her out. He looked like a criminal, but why were they looking for him at her office? Did this have something to do with Gerard's handling of the books?

Later, Gerard called in. Amanda told him about the visit and the picture. He was shocked. He asked, "Was it someone you recognized?"

"Hell, no. It was some guy with a beard and these heavy out-of-style glasses. He looked like a sex offender. I mean, that was the impression I got."

"Did they leave a copy of the photo? What else did they say?"

"They kept it. When they found out no one else was in the office, they left. They acted like they had wasted their time."

"You're right, Amanda. They're probably canvassing the neighborhood looking for some sicko child molester."

Amanda asked when he'd be back. He said three days. She told him she missed him and asked if he wanted to get together that night. Gerard told her he would call just before his return flight.

Gerard was panic-stricken. The agents were looking for him. That alone told him the case against him was never closed. How could they have traced him to Sarasota? Something didn't add up.

Gerard shuffled into the small hotel restaurant and spent the next two hours trying to unravel this mystery. He was torn between fleeing the country again, and waiting to see what happened next. He was so settled into his lifestyle in southwest Florida, that it was impossible to quickly liquidate and run. His only choice was to sit tight for the time being.

He called The Brazilian at the private number and left an urgent message.

A short time later, he got his call. "Mr. Morbus, Diego. How can I help you?"

Gerard explained the FBI. "They may have found me. What should I do?"

"Do nothing, Mr. Morbus. They could be watching. It may be an attempt to flush you out. Let me make some calls and see what I can learn. Meanwhile, do not withdraw any money from your bank. Wait for my call."

Despite the air-conditioning, Gerard was still sweating through his designer shirt. He felt better knowing that Diego Santos could help him.

The return call came that night. "Gerard, here's what I have been able to learn so far. Your case was never closed. It is not active. I cannot understand why the FBI is making inquiries about Harold Payne. It does not appear to be a serious threat. There is nothing imminent that I can uncover. Go about your business without change until I learn more."

Diego's report eased his panic, but the incident left a deep-seated fear that everything could unravel.

76

Dancing in the Dark

The morning he was due back, Gerard called Amanda to order in some dinner from Valentino's. He said to expect him about 7. She could hear the upbeat tone and was sure it was his anticipation of seeing her. He was looking forward to wine, dinner, and sex. He was also elated that he finally closed a solo deal. He was looking forward to celebrating. He also instructed her to have Petey come to the office the next day to detail the Aston Martin.

Instead of ordering from Valentino's, Amanda had arranged for a catered dinner to be prepared by the chef at Prestancia Country Club. She also ordered a magnum of Dom Perignon. Amanda even bought some candles, lighting them up on the conference table. And she charged everything on the company credit card Gerard had given her.

Knowing that Gerard was away and expected sometime over the next few days, Salete watched the office like a hawk. She wasn't sure if he would return a day or two earlier than scheduled, so she drove by each evening, but his car wasn't there, even though Amanda had worked late each day.

Then on the third night, when she drove by, she saw both cars. She parked across the street, watching the office, and about 9 the lights went off. She pulled into the street, ready to drive away as soon as she saw someone leave. After a few minutes, she realized that no one was coming out, and that whatever the two occupants were doing, they were doing it in the dark.

She drove home and after about an hour, got into bed and waited for Gerard. He finally came in about 1, greeted her, and undressed. When he kissed her goodnight, she smelled Amanda's unmistakable fragrance.

The evidence of infidelity was irrefutable. Salete had known since the beginning that Gerard was incapable of true love. At first, he tried diligently to please her, but in the end, his soulless character emerged. She could no longer spend her days alone and her nights unfulfilled. She had to move on.

77

Brotherly Love

When Diego arrived in Sarasota, he went directly to Salete's house for lunch and was angered by her distraught, depressed condition. "What happened to my beautiful sister? With all the luxury that surrounds you, why are you so unhappy?"

She cried, and he hugged her, saying, "Tell me everything."

Salete explained how they arrived in Sarasota, and how happy she had been living in this wonderful house in a city that was so beautiful. It was such an adventure furnishing and decorating it. As she said this, he was looking around, awed by the treasures that adorned the walls and shelves.

Questioning her, Salete described Gerard's disinterest, which had carried over from São Paulo. He had too much energy to sit around, and after so many years of winding down and decompressing, he had been looking for some new stimulation, which he couldn't find in Brazil.

Coming to America was challenging for them. Her insurance money that provided more than half the funds they had. And living in Sarasota was far more expensive than Brazil. She had used her money to buy the house in a cash transaction. It was in her name only. As a fugitive, Gerard was afraid of being traced through their homeownership and then arrested.

When they moved to the states, he consulted for companies. It was the first time in years he had energy. At the same time, she struggled for interests to motivate her. She tried to build a decorating and furnishing service in

Florida but had difficulty attracting customers. With their roles now reversed after moving from one country to another, and to a different culture, their relationship slowly broke down and deteriorated.

Salete explained they had become two strangers living in the same house. Gerard was so obsessed with building this consulting business and to accumulate a personal fortune that he completely ignored her needs, both mental and physical.

Diego said he had taken some action as a first step to frighten Gerard. Her sad story confirmed to him this was the right move. He explained that he had made an anonymous call to the FBI regarding Harold Payne's whereabouts.

This surprised Salete, and she wondered how this would affect her plans. During the previous days, after confirming Gerard's infidelity, she had devised a way to escape her dilemma.

Salete told him, "I recently have discovered he is having sexual companionship with other woman who works in office. And because of that, now he completely ignores me."

Diego shouted, "I will kill this unfaithful pig. I have warned him not to mistreat my sister. And he knows what I am capable of."

"Diego, *por favor*, this not about revenge. I need to get away from his unhappiness. Geraldo, he is lonely man. He cannot help it. There is no love in his heart. Me, I am warm person with strong need for love. This hollow person, he not capable of making me happy."

Salete then described her plan and what she needed Diego to do. Timing was critical.

He agreed to help make it happen. But he was disappointed in her lenient attitude towards Gerard. And he vowed that, despite her wishes, he would make him pay for hurting his sister.

78

Suspicions Aroused

Continuing their decades-long tradition of Friday date nights, Powers took Elisa to Underground to enjoy a quiet dinner and a bottle of wine. That night, restauranteur Jon Mills made the rounds of the diners. When he saw Powers, he came over and greeted him, saying, "I saw your partner Gerard last week at my other location, Rosemary Sunset. He brought me outside to show me his new Aston Martin. Bloody wow, what a set of wheels. And he must have been wearing a thousand-dollar tailored suit. You blokes must be pulling in a fortune."

Powers was taken aback and stammered that sales were accelerating rapidly. Angered by Gerard's excessive show of wealth, while his own compensation was denied, he decided to investigate.

On Monday, after checking on Gerard's travel schedule, he went to the office and spoke to Amanda. He asked her to download all the latest financial reports. Amanda adamantly refused. "Gerard does not allow anyone in the company reviewing the books, except when he sends out shareholder reports."

"Look Amanda, I founded this damn company and I hired Gerard. So, get me those damn reports."

"I'm sorry, Dave. I have my orders. Get him to approve it and I'll print any report you want."

After he left, Powers called Keyes and told him about his conversation with the restauranteur and his subsequent trip to the office. Keyes agreed with Powers, and later, he phoned and asked her to prepare the most recent financial reports for his investor presentation he was making. But again, Amanda refused. He called Gerard. His call was not returned.

Later, Gerard called in, and Amanda told him about the encounters with Powers and Keyes. He realized he had to quash the inquiry. "You did good, honey. I am impressed with your initiative and quick thinking. You can bet I'll reward your loyalty when I get back. In the meantime, I'll send you a memo to forward to all the shareholders under my name. See you in a couple of days."

Gerard then dictated the memo and sent it to her for distribution:

To All Shareholders,

Occasionally, some of you ask for interim reports on our status. While I understand your interest, I have requested the bookkeeper not to share financial information with any of the shareholders. The reason is the same as every corporation. Raw data between quarters can often be misleading, as it is incomplete. Rather than raise anyone's expectations, or deliver negative news, I have told her shareholders would receive only quarterly reports, once the accountant has reviewed and adjusted them for any open items or journal entries.

I trust you understand and agree with these standard business practices. I can tell you in this current quarter we will register our largest volume of sales yet. However, with rapidly accelerating business, cash flow drops precipitously. But we are in the right direction.

Gerard Morbus, Chairman and CEO

After reading the communication, Powers called Keyes and said Gerard's rationale was a smokescreen. Keyes agreed. They were both concerned about Gerard's sudden show of wealth and his lack of candor on the finance reports. Keyes promised Powers he would investigate.

Following the call, Keyes felt a pang of divided loyalties. He agreed with Powers' assessment of the profit drop and Gerard's flaunting success. Yet, he was now in a business

214

relationship that Gerard initiated, and would provide him with a substantial windfall.

He expected checks from the property owners based on their savings. He had been told the savings had been exceeding the estimates and delivering a larger payout. The firm received more than expected in the first year of installation, and now Keyes and the other partners would get their payout. He didn't want to rock the boat, and trigger Gerard's anger, but he would have to do some quiet investigating.

79

Cooking the Books

Gerard returned to town a little earlier than previous trips. Some time had passed since the FBI visit, and he was relaxing. There wasn't any further news from Diego, and maybe no pending threat existed.

He and Amanda sat in his office and he told her about his plans. He was making her a vice-president and giving her a raise. He also promised her a company car at the beginning of the next quarter. Excited, she straddled his lap and planted her tongue in his mouth. She began rocking back and forth, giving him a lap dance. Just before he came, she climbed off him, unzipped his fly and sucked his erect penis.

When he recovered with the boost from Viagra, she helped slide his pants off and again mounted him, this time with him inside her. She rocked back and forth gently, controlling the pace until he was stiff again. She then increased the rhythm, pounding harder and harder until they both reached an explosive orgasm. She then rested her head on his chest without removing his penis.

Laying against him, she looked back on their romance and thought about how the intimacy had improved from the crude beginning until now when it was becoming so much more of a love relationship.

Minutes later, they went into the restrooms and cleaned up. Gerard took her out to dinner, then drove home.

The next morning, he instructed her about modifying the bookkeeping process. He told her to change the posting on certain items to different account numbers and move his credit card expenses to the installation account. He then had her move some other categories. These changes helped to enhance the profit shown on the financial statements for their installation business, as it hid his lavish spending. He knew at some point the accountant would uncover the errors, but he would deal with that later.

80

Deadbeat Client

When Gerard walked into the office in the morning, Keyes was waiting. Sensing something was wrong, he went on the offensive. "Angelo, you just can't show up any time you want. I'm so busy; my whole day is booked. I only have a few minutes. What's the problem? Didn't you get laid last night? Hahaha."

Angelo's anger was now boiling over, "I'll tell you what you can do for me. You can get your fucking client to pay me from his water savings."

"What the fuck are you talking about? We got paid for our entire period, and it was far more than we expected."

"Well, maybe that's the problem. Your client decided he paid more than enough for the installation and interest to date, so he's now going to keep all the savings for himself, and not pay us the third-year's payout."

"Keep in mind that he's your client too. He has a separate contract with you to pay you the savings for the third year to cover the interest on the financing."

"I told him that, but he's dug in. He said he's not paying another dime. He told me to get the interest money from you, as HydroDyne made a fortune on the deal. I argued with him for an hour and he won't budge. I don't know what to do."

"There's only one thing left to do. Sue the fuck. You have a contract. He must pay you."

"Can't you talk to him? If I sue, it will cost a bundle and take a year. And there goes my profit."

"Okay, I will call him. But if I don't get anywhere, it's your problem. I'll let you know. Now, get the fuck out of here. I've got work to do."

81

Joyless Sex

Gerard next flew to Costa Rica for some rest and relaxation. He needed time to develop a long-term plan to capitalize on his position. He had been using all the usual tricks to embezzle money from the company, but he now had to develop a method to use the firm's assets for his benefit and grow rich.

He thought about the profile makeup of the investors and formulated an idea. With just a few exceptions, they were all in their mid- to late-seventies and were impatient for their return on investment. And this fact spawned his scheme.

He needed a couple of critical steps to complete his structure. First, he had to set up a second set of books and open an account at another bank. Then he had to get Emilio to quit. He had already pushed Lawson, Park, and Newman out, and he marginalized Powers and the others, so the rest would be easy.

The hard part of the sting was to set up the buyout and arrange the timing.

Once he completed the plan, it was time to unwind and feed his libido. He went to the bar where all the prostitutes hung out, and started drinking. He studied the girls and picked out the most beautiful woman there. Speaking in Spanish, Gerard got her a drink and said he needed lots of love. "I need love of two women, beautiful like you."

"*No hay problema, señor.*"

Gerard left with the two attractive ladies of the night. When he got back to the mansion, he saw them in the brighter light and realized they looked much better in the dark bar.

The threesome spent the next few hours performing every possible combination of oral and penetrating sex. After their multiple faked orgasms, and his Viagra-assisted three climaxes, he was done. By the time they left, he was exhausted and covered with bodily fluids.

As soon as he closed the door, Gerard raced into the bathroom and took a long shower, scrubbing his genitals and his face, until they were raw. As he toweled off, he alternately gargled and spit out mouthwash multiple times whispering the popular slogan *Listerine kills millions of germs on contact*. He just didn't want anything dying in his mouth.

82

Getting Intoxicated

Back in Sarasota after his Latin American trip, Gerard was energized and excited. He met with Amanda and got her started on his new plan. He had her open a bank account at a small Bradenton bank up Tamiami Trail. And on his instructions, she bought another computer. He advised her to set up a new company in QuickBooks, using all the same information as the original, but with a different password. She also keyed in the new bank for payables and receivables.

Gerard later explained which customer orders to bill through the new company and to deposit those corresponding payments into the new bank account. He also had her issue the two of them an additional 500 shares of stock from the employee pool.

Amanda was sure what he had her doing was illegal. And although she was apprehensive, she found it thrilling because Gerard was making her part of his master plan. His long-range vision impressed her and just how he knew how to put everything in place. Then he took her to the Lexus dealer and leased her a new ES350.

She had no idea of the outcome of Gerard's plan, yet she trusted him and was certain it would be life-changing for her and for the company. With caution to the wind, she now had a purpose in life, something with a substantial long-term reward that was materializing now. Her participation gave her the sense of being an integral part of the caper, and his partner in this clandestine adventure. The power was intoxicating.

83

Firing the Clients

The weekly installation report noted a few of the properties installing the system with their maintenance staff had recurring problems. These ranged from disappointing utility savings to water flow issues. And sometimes, both.

Emilio had a meeting scheduled with the regional VP of one of his largest clients, a REIT that owned and managed hundreds of rental property locations in several states. Seeing the opportunity to expedite his plan, Gerard decided to attend, at the company's headquarters in Fort Lauderdale. The VP sat on one side of the conference table, flanked by the two maintenance supervisors of the affected properties, both of whom were Hispanic. Also, in attendance were the two property managers. Gerard and Emilio sat on the other side.

Both technicians explained they had been trained by HydroDyne to install the complex system, and they followed the process precisely. The VP had a stack of utility bills showing no savings, and in some months, a slight increase. Passing them around, he concluded the units were defective and he wanted them replaced.

Emilio tried to respond, but Gerard took his forearm to stop him. He turned to the VP, "Our systems are made to exacting specifications, and every single one is factory tested before it leaves the facility. So, it can't be the fault of the equipment."

"Mr. Morbus, I'm sure you understand there is a vast difference between controlled factory testing and field utilization. Your units need to be either repaired or replaced. And it's not a request, it's a demand."

Gerard fired back, "Look, you pompous jerk. There's nothing wrong with my equipment. It has to be the way your dumb fucking Spicks installed it. We aren't replacing a damn thing."

No one had ever spoken to the executive like that. He stood, stared at Gerard and said, "You apologize to my men for that slur." And turning to Emilio, he said, "I'm sorry, Emilio. I cannot work with any person as arrogant and bigoted as your CEO. I'm canceling every order we have on the books. And I'll expect you to remove and credit us for any equipment we find defective. This meeting is over. Now please leave."

When they left the building, Emilio was so angry that he could have punched Gerard. "How could you say something so stupid to my biggest client? And to make it that much worse, you insult his employees. What were you thinking?"

"Emilio, don't question me. I was right. The fault lies with those two fucking Cubans. They are uneducated jerks, just like everyone else from the islands. They can barely speak English, so how can they follow directions? And, if you disagree, it's because you're one of them."

"Well, fuck you! I'm not putting up with this shit. I'm done. Get yourself another uneducated *Spick* to sell your defective products."

As Emilio walked away, Gerard thought his plan was working out easier than he expected. And despite the intentional play to get rid of the client, they convinced him he was justified in his criticism of the VP and the two maintenance assholes. Pushing Emilio to resign this quickly was an unexpected bonus.

Gerard returned to his car and called Emilio's client in Orlando. This company also had hundreds of properties mostly in Florida, and they were all low-rise to mid-rise structures.

He spoke to the facilities officer who registered a complaint about the system performance. It was nearly the same script as the one in his previous meeting upstairs. And the results were the same. Gerard knew all the hot buttons to push and he immediately got HydroDyne fired from this account as well.

84

Another One Drops

On Gerard's way back to the office, Keyes called.

"Gerard, I haven't heard back from you. Did you resolve the payment problem that we spoke about?"

"I called him, and you're right, the prick said he will not pay either one of us any more money. We're both stuck, and will have to sue to collect."

"How could you let this happen? He's your client. We're just a sub-contractor to facilitate the financing of your sale. I expect HydroDyne to make good on the money we are owed."

"Fuck you, Angelo. You've been in business long enough to know that there is always a risk. Sue them if you have to, but we're not paying you anything."

"I'll be in your office tomorrow morning. And we damn well better get this worked out."

Gerard hung up.

The exchange left Keyes fuming. Maybe Powers was right. Gerard Morbus was not someone you could trust. He was getting his money. There was no doubt about that.

Keyes was camped out in front of the office when Gerard opened up the next morning. Gerard could sense the anger and knew he'd have his hands full.

They sat across from each other in the conference room and Keyes pulled a stack of papers out of a file folder. "If the client reneges on the loan, HydroDyne is on the hook. I have the contract here to prove it."

Seeing all the documentation, Gerard said, "I don't care what the paperwork says, we're not paying their debt."

"Then I'm moving ahead immediately with a lawsuit against the company. I can put a lien on your bank account, and probably get a summary judgment."

"Think carefully about this. If you sue the company, I will call in your stock. And I don't think you want that."

Keyes stood up, incredulous. "You refuse to pay me and now you're threatening me? Well, fuck you Morbus! You don't know what you're up against."

It took Keyes the rest of the day to calm down and think about his dilemma. He was sure he could collect the $150,000 debt from HydroDyne, but he'd have to sell his shares back. Without an accurate financial statement, he didn't know the value of his shares. Gerard's opaque management made it impossible to make an informed decision.

He was between a rock and a hard-ass.

85

Setting up the Sting

Jon Mills was still renting the condo from Gerard when he got the call.

"Jon, this is Gerard. How's your new house coming along?"

"Despite all the rain delays, we expect to be complete and get our CO in the next two months. Why, do you need the condo back?"

"No. Two months is fine. But I have an opportunity you'll be interested in. It goes beyond the small investment you made in the company. Can we meet?"

"I have seen how your company has grown and the success you are enjoying. So, yes, I would like to hear what you have in mind."

They met that night. Gerard explained that he was going to flip the company, buy out the investors, and reorganize it. Jon could become a 25% owner of the new company with Gerard. He would only have to put up $250,000, but he would have to be the face of the new firm that bought out the shareholders.

Confused, Mills asked, "Where do we get the money to buy back all the stock? I just spent a bloody fortune building this house on Lido Key for my wife."

"You'll need $250K. There are about a million shares outstanding, plus ours. They're worth between $6 and $8 a pop. I've just created a panic and you'll be the white knight to step in and buy up the shares for 50 cents each. And if they resist, you'll go as high as 75 cents."

"Now, get your hands on $250K, and I'll come up with whatever amount we'll need to acquire all the stock.

"It will take me about a year to get the company back to peak performance, and we can flip it for a minimum of $5 million. Are you in?"

"$5 million? Bloody right, I am!"

86

Outsmarting the FBI

Gerard directed Amanda to send out a letter to the investors.

To All Shareholders:

Despite our recent successes, we are facing a situation that is threatening the survival of the company. There is a serious flaw in our system that eliminates its water-saving performance. Many of our clients demand we replace or remove the equipment.

This effort will easily bankrupt our struggling company. Two of our largest clients have already terminated their relationship with us. Because of this disastrous turn of events, our key sales rep, Emilio Lopez has resigned. I believe he went back to Cuba.

To salvage our collective investment, I have uncovered an investor who has a serious interest in purchasing the company, but he is demanding an immediate response. He claims his engineering team can overcome the flaws in our system. He has a companion product to sell to our customer base, making the acquisition attractive to him.

After spending significant time in the field, I am convinced the cost to overcome these problems is staggering. Given that, I urge we negotiate the best deal so we can come away with most or all of our initial investment intact.

I'll meet with this investor early next week, hoping we can strike a deal before these design flaws destroy our company.

Gerard Morbus, Chairman and CEO

As soon as it went out, Gerard left the office again to make a call on one other client who was having problems.

This one was a referral from an investor. Gerard felt he could use this customer to stoke the investor panic he was trying to create with all the investors. He planned to take a similar approach as he did with the other two clients. He would use softer rhetoric.

That afternoon, Amanda went to the bank to make a deposit and was startled when she saw the same two FBI men in the branch manager's office. She quickly left without being seen by them and called Gerard.

Surprised that they were at the company's bank branch, he quickly recovered, thinking it was probably a coincidence, and not to be concerned.

Pulling into a nearby diner, Gerard was shaken and hyperventilating. As he calmed down, he rethought his plans. He sat in a booth fuming over this new complication and reviewed the entire caper. Since The Brazilian had not called with any update, he thought he was still relatively safe. But he had to have a backup plan in case the FBI made a move on him.

After mulling over all his options, an idea came to him. He was about to pull off this deal with Mills, and that train was well out of the station. If the oven got too hot, he could easily swindle Mills out of all the money in the firm's accounts, unload the inventory, and maybe even dump his stock. He would need Diego's help once again, but he had lots of options to pull off another multimillion-dollar heist.

His first step was to have Amanda park even more money in the new accounts. And once the takeover was in progress, he'd call Diego and start moving $100,000 at a time out of the country. If there was no threat, he'd move the money back when he and Mills bought out the investors. Otherwise, he'd use the money for his escape. Nobody had the cunning to beat him, not even the FBI.

87

Pushed Over the Edge

Angelo Keyes read the letter and immediately called Fred Bouie, a client he knew personally. "Fred, it's Angelo Keyes. I just got some disturbing news about a potential problem with the HydroDyne system. How is yours running?"

"Interesting you should call. My bookkeeper told me that the system isn't showing the savings we were getting in the beginning. What's wrong?"

"I don't know. But it sounds serious. I'll let you know when I find out more."

This was the piece of information Keyes needed to decide about the money he was owed. Instead of the stock soaring over the next few years, it was about to crash.

He called Gerard. "Your letter got my attention. The money I'm owed is more than my stock will be worth. I'm filing a claim against HydroDyne immediately. Prepare the paperwork to buy back my stock."

"I'll have the accountant prepare an accurate financial statement and determine the share value. I'll call you when the papers are ready."

Keyes knew he had to move fast. Between the debt owed and the value of the stock, it was a lot of money for the company to pay. And he needed to get his before it went broke.

Instead of being angry at Keyes, Gerard was delighted. This was one more crack in the dam that was about to burst. The plan was accelerating.

88

Bearer of Bad News

Gerard arrived at the client's property in Des Moines and was immediately ushered into the office of the owner. He knew he would have to make a slight change in his tactic. He was in the heartland, so his big city, profanity-laced hard sell would turn this bible-reading country hick off in a nanosecond. Bluster was certainly not the way to go, as the client was a friend of an investor. And the last thing Gerard needed was negative feedback getting to any of the shareholders.

Letting the customer make small talk allowed Gerard to create the bond needed to get his message across. After 10 minutes of weather, fishing, and the upcoming local art and craft festival, the owner got to the issue at hand, which was the poor performance of the system.

Listening to the customer's discontent for several minutes, Gerard said, "We haven't yet determined if there is any flaw in the equipment. We have received other complaints, but it will take several months to conduct all the research required to determine fault. In the meantime, since you did your installation, there is no warranty."

The owner was flabbergasted. "How could that be? We are certain that we installed the equipment precisely as the video shows. Don't you stand behind your products?"

"As I said, we have yet to find fault with the system. But we are working diligently. If it's the equipment, we'll stand behind it. I will report to you as soon as possible."

Concluding the meeting, Gerard left to return to Sarasota. But when he got to the airport, he changed his flight, booking a private jet to Las Vegas instead. He needed a change of scenery. And besides, it was too soon to return home to face the investors.

89

Fighting Back

When Powers got Gerard's report, he was incredulous. He was sure that the system was designed and built to function as specified. The gasket issue was an easy repair, although Gerard never implemented it. And Powers was convinced that was the problem.

There was more to this story than what the letter said. And why did Emilio resign? He was one of the most successful sales executives that Powers had ever encountered.

He tried to call Emilio, but the call went to voicemail. The voicemail message advised the callers that Emilio was in Cuba visiting family and wouldn't return for a few weeks. Hearing that, he did not leave a message.

Powers also called Gerard and his call went to voicemail. Not surprising.

He sent out an email blast of his own to all the investors.

Fellow Shareholders,

By now you have read Gerard's report about the perceived flaw in the equipment, and the urgent need for us to abandon the company.

I am writing to implore you to step back and wait until we have all the facts to make an informed decision. The company has been in business for 10 years, having survived all this time. Why should we be forced to sell in one week? I am convinced that our system is functional and sound, and we can overcome any issues that are emerging. If there are problems at any properties, they were most likely caused by

235

installation, and not the product. And if it was product-related, it would be the problem-prone gasket.

Tell Gerard we are not ready to sell without conclusive evidence of a significant issue with our system.

Dave Powers

Showing Gerard's email and his response to Elisa, he explained, "This is a scam. If Gerard pulls it off, we're ruined."

"You've got stop him. He'll take our company away."

Hugging his wife who he loved so dearly he confessed, "Elisa, I'm truly frightened. I don't know how to stop him. We've got to shatter his plan."

"We have faced similar catastrophes and you've never let us down. It won't happen now."

90

Dire Warning

Salete continued to monitor Gerard's encounters with Amanda, as she put her plan together.

Her first step was to go to the bank and open a line of credit. She requested the loan using the house as collateral. Since there was no mortgage, the loan officer determined the line could easily go as high as $500,000. Seeing the large balances and activity in their checking account, he asked its purpose. She explained she was opening a furniture and décor service, where she needed to stock a warehouse with furnishings, artwork, and decorative accessories.

They approved the loan the following day, although she was not ready to draw down on the funds.

Salete then drove to the office and marched in the front door, where she was greeted by Amanda.

"Mrs. Morbus, how are you? Gerard is not here. He's still out of town and not expected until next week. Anything I can do?"

"Amanda, I know Geraldo is not at office. And I am aware also, of what you and he do."

Hiding her surprise, Amanda replied, "I have no idea what you're talking about."

"Oh, you do. You having sex with him every time he come home. Screwing."

"Mrs. Morbus, that is a terrible thing to say. I'm the office manager here. And very professional. I don't fool around with married men."

It was then that Salete noticed the Prada bag on the credenza behind Amanda's desk. "How do you afford handbag so expensive?"

"My boyfriend bought it for me at a bazaar when he was in Europe."

Drilling into her eyes, Salete hissed, "Your lies mean nothing. I know. I give you one week to leave this job. Go away and do not come back. This is only warning you will get."

Salete turned on her heels and left. Amanda was so shaken she could barely breathe. *How did she know? Had Gerard told her about them? Was he playing her?* This was confusing. She decided she wouldn't tell him about this encounter until after he returned to the office. And then she would see how he treated her when they were alone.

91

Rolling the Dice
May 2019, Las Vegas, NV

Arriving at McCarran Airport, Gerard turned his phone on and was greeted with an email from Jon Mills who requested a call back right away. The message contained a copy of Powers' email that went to every investor but Gerard. He swore aloud and wondered when he was going to be rid of this persistent pain in his ass. Powers was like a recurring case of the clap.

He had Amanda send out a message to the shareholders advising them that the company was being sued over a financing dispute, and they were certain to lose that case. He added that the lawsuit may spook the purchaser, so they had to move quickly to accept the deal.

Gerard then called Mills back and instructed him to email the HydroDyne shareholders an ultimatum to accept his offer or he would withdraw it.

A short time later, Gerard got an email from the investor whose friend owned the property in Des Moines. That owner had called complaining about the product, which threw the shareholder into a panic. He urged Gerard to take advantage of the offer and sell the company.

Gerard forwarded this email to all the other investors, along with a proxy form to vote for acceptance of the offer.

Knowing that the sheep would stampede off the cliff, he went down to the hotel bar and ordered a double shot of their best single malt scotch.

After a couple of drinks, he felt lucky, and wandered into the casino.

At the craps table, he rolled the dice and hit a hot streak. With nothing to lose, he kept doubling up on each roll. He walked away with over $9,000.

The win at the tables made him feel invincible and more confident than ever. This sign of good fortune convinced him he was about to close this deal and end up with the entire company. And that made him feel ecstatic.

92

Escape from Paradise
May 2019, Sarasota, FL

Diego had one final meeting with Salete before she left, and he questioned her on all the steps he had recommended.

She had cashed in all their CDs and deposited the funds in their money market savings account. She withdrew the entire $500,000 line of credit and moved that to the same account. The total came to well over $3 million. He gave her an account number at a bank in the Caymans and told her to wire all the funds, keeping about $8,000 in cash with her. He would then transfer all the money to a bank account in São Paulo.

Diego then gave her a one-way plane ticket to Aruba, where she had a reservation at the Marriott Hotel. It was a huge, busy hotel, where she would not be noticed. The room charges were paid for one night. In the morning, a car would take her to a private plane at the airport.

Salete shared her conversation with Gerard's bookkeeper and her warning to *a prostituta*. She told Diego that she had thoroughly frightened the woman, and she would leave the company before Gerard returned. She also explained that Gerard would be back in town in 48 hours, and would be at the office well into that evening. She must leave before he arrived.

Her only concern was Gerard coming home early and somehow finding out all the money was gone. It was a very remote possibility, as he never looked at their accounts. She didn't want to take that chance. Once he realized she had left for good, he would then check the accounts. He'd discover he was broke.

Salete reiterated that she wanted Diego to make sure that Gerard understood that there was no reconciliation. He should not try to find her. "My brother, put the fear of God in him, but *por favor*, there is no need to hurt him."

Telling her not to worry, Diego handed her a pouch that contained a new identity, a credit card, and a cell phone. He kissed her and said, "I will take care of everything here as you requested. I will make sure he does not come home before you leave. And I look forward to seeing you soon in São Paulo where you will resume the life you miss so much."

93

Last Ditch Attempt
May 2019, Las Vegas, NV

Enjoying breakfast in bed in his luxury suite at Bellagio on the Strip, Gerard was tracking the proxies arriving by email. By the time he ate, and got dressed, he had nearly enough shares pledged, plus his, to close the deal.

He returned to the casino to see if his luck at the tables would translate to a done deal on the company before he left town.

He wandered around the casino like he owned the place, trying baccarat, poker, and the slots. By noon, he had lost nearly all the winnings from the previous night. Shrugging off this change of luck, he thought to himself, *this is why I'm so successful. I'm bulletproof and can overcome any challenge.*

He left for the airport and caught his flight home. He still was a little short on the share votes he needed.

In the meantime, Powers called every shareholder to persuade them to decline the deal. But he wasn't succeeding. The momentum was going the opposite way and he was unsure that he would carry the day. He was close to having enough votes to block Gerard's deal, but he was doubtful that he could get the additional votes needed to stop him.

When Gerard got to McCarran Airport, he checked in with Amanda. She told him it was all quiet. He instructed her to schedule Petey to come over the next day to detail the Aston Martin. After he hung up, he checked his email, and there was a voicemail from a shareholder who had not yet voted. The investor was in Europe and would be back over the weekend. He told Gerard that he would hand deliver his proxy on Monday morning. That put the vote in Gerard's favor. Once he voted his shares, he would have won the proxy battle.

The revenge would be sweet. He was now able to fuck over Dave Powers, Angelo Keyes, and the rest of those asshole investors. They kept interfering with his management of the firm with their constant questioning of his brilliant decisions. It didn't have to be this way. He would have been comfortable with all of them making a good return on their investment, while he took the lion's share which he so well deserved. But they tried to obstruct his plan, and now they would end up with nothing.

At about the same time, Powers got a return phone call from Emilio, who had just returned from Cuba. Being an investor, he had received all the emails from Gerard, Mills, and Powers, and he was angry. Having figured out Gerard's scheme, he explained what really happened at his client's office. Powers made an appointment to meet him for a drink that night.

Before Gerard left the airport, a text came in from Powers.

Gerard, you must halt this sale immediately. If you don't, I will stop you. I am getting an affidavit from Emilio. With that, my lawyer will ask a judge to issue a restraining order to end this charade. And if that doesn't stop you, I will find a way to hurt you in a way that will make you wish you never tried to steal our company. This is not an idle threat!

In a nanosecond, Gerard's euphoria imploded and was replaced by a violent temper tantrum. He screamed at his phone, "Powers, you have fucked with me for the last time!"

His booming voice echoed inside so that everyone in the crowded terminal stopped and turned to stare at him. Embarrassed, he slunk away.

94

A Wing and a Prayer
June 2019, Sarasota, FL

When Powers didn't hear back from Gerard, he called his friend Bobby Torq, one of the original investors. Torq was a wealthy entrepreneur who invested in the company as a way to help his friend, rather than looking for a huge return on his investment.

Torq had just returned to his home in New Jersey from a lengthy vacation in New Zealand and Australia. He had a lot of questions about the communications from Gerard and was glad Powers reached out to him.

After hearing about how Gerard was manipulating the clients and causing Emilio to resign, Torq was furious. "Dave, how can we stop him?"

"I'm not sure, but we have to move fast. I expect a call back from Emilio after he talks to his big client who fired us.

"I am getting an attorney to file a motion to halt the sale to this mysterious investor. If you'll help, wire me $10,000 right away. We'll also need a big chunk to buy out Gerard and take back the company. Can you help me do all that?"

"I'll do whatever is necessary to get rid of this parasite. Is it worth saving, or are we too late?"

"We've taken several major hits from Gerard's plundering and self-dealing. And it still has been wildly successful. I hope Emilio's return will help us regain what we lost, and then move forward. I may be able to recover a couple of big clients Gerard sabotaged. That, plus a simple marketing program will get it done."

"Go for it, Dave. I've got your back, even though I think it's a long shot to pull it off."

Next, Powers phoned Newman and asked her for a good litigation attorney. He filled her in on what had been transpiring. As a minor shareholder, she knew of the communications from Gerard, but did not know the depth of his misconduct with Emilio and the clients.

She gave him the name of the best lawyer she knew for this type of lawsuit. She wished him luck, yet shared her serious doubts about the success of the endeavor. Newman also feared that her transgressions may surface after the dust settled.

Powers met with Ron Klein the next day, and explained his predicament. Klein agreed to take the case and would file the motion with the court the following morning.

When Powers got back to his home office, he heard from Emilio's client, Les Winters. When asked for the details of HydroDyne's termination, Winters was more than willing to share the specifics of the unbelievable scene in his conference room.

Hearing the story firsthand, Powers was shocked. He asked Winters if he would consider testifying against Gerard, if it came to that.

"Mr. Powers, it was a painful and disturbing experience, but I am not inclined to appear in court, as much as I would like to burn your Neanderthal CEO."

Powers asked Winters if he would resume business with HydroDyne, if Gerard were terminated and Emilio came back. Winters said he would consider it, but would not commit.

It was a rollercoaster few days for Powers, but overall, he was encouraged that the fight was not over. He called each investor, asking them to withdraw their proxy. Most said they would wait to see what happened with the restraining order, but others were now vacillating. It may be a long shot, but there was still a possibility he could save his company.

95

Familiar Surroundings
June 2019, São Paulo, Brazil

Leaving the beautiful home in Sarasota with all its painful memories relieved Salete's fear and anxiety. She was free of Gerard's impersonal treatment and infidelity. He would be shocked and livid when he discovered she took all the money. Salete was also certain that he would not try to find her. Diego would convince him to walk away and forget her.

Salete's flight to Aruba, with a stopover in Houston, was uneventful. When she arrived, she took a taxi to the hotel. Once in her room, she ordered dinner from room service and then went to bed.

After a restless night at the Marriott, Salete got dressed in the outfit Diego told her to wear. She put on the wig, her sunglasses, and a scarf. She then went down to the lobby, had a cup of coffee, and walked out to the front entrance. A limousine awaited, with the driver holding a sign that read Almeida.

The driver took her bag, and Salete got in the back seat. They drove the short distance to the airport where the private planes were parked. He dropped her off in front of a waiting Lear jet.

The plane promptly took off. And as it flew high above Venezuela, it changed course and went to São Paulo.

At the small private airport, a taxi rushed Salete to an upscale, residential neighborhood, where her new apartment was located. It was sparsely furnished. As she looked around the rooms, she saw the flat as a canvas that was anticipating an artist to paint it. She couldn't wait to begin to decorate this beautiful condo, her new home.

Salete walked out to the balcony and looked over the neighborhood in this exclusive part of the city. The familiar sounds and pungent fragrances drifted up and welcomed her. She was home, and her new life awaited her.

There was a 10-year hole in her life, and she was determined to make up for that time. And for her, there was no place better to start than São Paulo.

96

Justice Served
June 2019, Sarasota, FL

Gerard boarded the Gulfstream jet and found only a few passengers aboard as he took his seat. The flight attendant greeted him and offered a drink. He looked up and was struck by her beauty. She had movie-star looks and a perfectly sculpted body. Her high heels enhanced the shape of her legs.

When she brought his scotch, Gerard engaged her in conversation. He was enthralled by her broad smile, huge green eyes and spiked blond hair. And he kept glancing at the bit of cleavage showing above her open blouse. When asked what he did, Gerard boasted about his sales triumphs and prowess running a successful company in Sarasota. As they talked, he wondered if she was a member of the Mile-High Club.

As the plane approached the coast of Florida, the attendant came around and urgently told each passenger to buckle up and stow their belongings, as there was rough weather ahead. Gerard noticed she was now wearing sneakers instead of the heels she had on earlier. Maybe this was serious.

They hit the turbulence almost immediately. The plane rocked and then plunged a thousand feet. Rain deluged the sky as lightning struck all around them. The plane reacted like it was being punched by giant clouds. It rocked constantly and changed elevation up and down by thousands of feet. One dive was so steep they could see the ground before the plane recovered and regained altitude. Gerard feared for his life.

The scotch and food in Gerard's stomach did not stay put, and it worked its way up. He needed to get to the bathroom, a short, but impossible journey. The barf bag was his only choice as he vomited multiple times.

After circling in the storm for an hour, the pilot got permission to land. When the plane parked at the private terminal, Gerard relaxed. He had never been so frightened in his life. He was drenched in sweat from the vertigo and the thought of dying.

Gerard staggered off the plane and went to his car. He sat in the driver's seat and tried to settle his dizziness. He opened the door and vomited again. After that, he felt better and drove to the office.

Gerard parked in his usual spot behind the building. On the drive back, he thought about Powers' text, and blew off any thought a restraining order would be granted. Feeling better, he marched into the office like he owned the place. He was ready to consummate the deal. He couldn't contain his excitement.

When Amanda trotted to greet him, he hugged her, picked her up and kissed her.

He said, "Everything is falling into place. There will soon be an eruption that will change the world for us."

Amanda had a bottle of Dom Perignon ready to celebrate. Sipping their first glasses, he told her about the vote, and explained how they would take over the company. They'd cash in.

"I did it, Amanda. One by one, I got rid of them all. It's like an executive bone yard out there."

Amanda was excited, and felt positive about Gerard's plans for her, yet she was still apprehensive. She had to clear the air, so she told him about Salete's visit to the office, and her threat.

Gerard put down his glass, and paused. "Honey, let me tell you about Salete. I met her when I moved to Brazil. She helped me get established there and I became attracted to her. Eventually we fell in love."

"I can see how that could happen. She's a very beautiful woman."

"Unfortunately, our cultural backgrounds are so different, that the relationship worked well in her world, but not here in mine. After we moved to this country, she found it difficult to gain acceptance, and grew withdrawn. It's sad, but it's the reality. And your sense of excitement has drawn me closer to you."

Amanda was now convinced that Gerard chose her over his wife. Feeling ecstatic and relieved, she stood up and took off her blouse, and then her skirt. She was wearing a new set of sexy black lingerie.

She then stood Gerard up and undressed him. When he was down to his tighty whities, the contrast was almost comical. She also knew not to take off his black socks.

Pushing him gently on the couch, she slid off his shorts and her panties, pulling him on top of her with their crotches in each other's faces. As they started oral sex, he got another wave of nausea. The vomit came fast and splattered all over Amanda's abdomen, crotch and thighs. He rolled over as she ran to the bathroom to clean herself off.

Suddenly, a loud explosion rocked the back of the building. Jumping up, Gerard screamed, "My Aston Martin!" The quick move caused the return of the dizziness, and he fell back on the couch.

The back of the warehouse blew in and a fireball raced between the drop ceiling and the roof. In seconds, burning debris rained down and there was fire everywhere. The flames spread throughout the building, and everything seemed to catch fire at once. It was a ravaging inferno.

Gerard staggered to his feet, reaching for his clothes, without bothering with his shoes. Ignoring Amanda, he stumbled towards the front door to save himself. It was too late. The intense heat and smoke were overwhelming. There was no escape. His hair caught fire and he fell down. He could hear Amanda screaming in the bathroom. The firestorm consumed them both in 90 seconds.

Gerard's last words: "Oh fuck. The Brazilian!"

Epilogue

HydroDyne Technologies

The fire left all the shareholders in mourning, as they recognized that their investment had gone up in smoke. There was nothing left of the building, including product inventory, furniture, files and computers. Everything was lost.

The fire was big news in the small town of Sarasota. Powers and his company were familiar to the editor of the regional business magazine, as there was a feature story about them when the firm was launched. Newspapers, TV, along with the other Gulf Coast media, covered the devastating news.

Facing nothing but ashes, Dave Powers was not ready to give up. He immediately took charge of the situation. He called Bobby Torq and asked him to come to Sarasota to help him with the salvage operation. He also called Emilio to join the team to rebuild the company.

He contacted Joe Floret for advice on recovering the computer files. Floret had helped set up the company's backup system when Lawson and Powers were the only employees. He checked the cloud system where the files were stored and found the account was intact.

When he called Powers, Floret asked if he knew the current password. Powers told him he only had the original password. Certain it had been changed multiple times over the years, he reluctantly gave it to Floret to start the recovery process.

An hour later, Floret called back. "Dave, you're not going to believe this. The original password is still good. I guess shit-for-brains Morbus never changed it."

"A better guess would be that he was unaware of the automatic backup."

With the data intact, Powers called the accounting firm, had them do a forensic accounting, and restructure the bookkeeping system. Unfortunately, the new computer that Amanda used for the clandestine accounts was not connected to the cloud. That data did not show up in the investigation.

When Angelo Keyes found out the about the effort to revive the company, he called Powers and demanded his stock buyback as promised. He explained about the Savings-Share finance company he set up at Gerard's urging, and how he had to sell his stock when the client wouldn't pay.

Angered, Powers told him he would buy back his shares for $1 per share, which was double what Gerard had offered the shareholders. And he strongly advised Keyes to take it or be investigated for his part in the demise of the company. Keyes accepted.

A week later, the president of the bank in Bradenton called Powers. He had read about the fire, and when nobody from the company took any action with the account at his bank, he followed up. Powers was shocked to learn about the account, with over $2 million in it.

Powers and Emilio hit the road within a week to salvage every client they could. Their success rate was just under 100%. They then contacted every prospect that Gerard had sabotaged and reconstructed the prospect lists that were deleted in Salesforce.

Powers launched a marketing campaign to reignite interest among them. This included public relations and social media. After advertising in The Wall Street Journal, he was able to place a feature story there that included case study data from a few of the REIT clients. Powers also added a feature to the website, where prospects could add their water use statistics and property details. The program would output the approximate savings in water volume and dollars.

In one year, they more than doubled the sales reached under Gerard's management, climbing to $9.70 million. And without his embezzlement and extravagance, gross profit surpassed 60%. They sold the company the following year for $16.5 million.

Dave Powers

After Powers sold the company to a private equity firm, he and Elisa retired. They bought a new home in a gated golf community in Sarasota. And they continued their Friday night dinner dates.

Within three months, he grew restless. Golf, tennis, and travel didn't come close to fulfilling his need for a business challenge. He joined Toastmasters and began public speaking. His pet topic was entrepreneurship. He frequently addressed business groups and service organizations and was a guest lecturer at college campuses.

His colorful career provided him a wealth of experiences, both positive and negative, all of which were learning experiences. Powers wrote books about the amazing events that he had encountered. He wrote them in the form of novels and self-help books.

Martha Billings

After the discovery of the stolen inventory, Martha Billings was devastated. Her only consolation was that her opinion of Harold Payne had been justified. She immediately called her attorney, Carleton Hanks, desperate for his help.

He calmly told her not to panic, that there would be a way to make some kind of recovery from the catastrophe. He found the insurance agent who provided the policies, and their umbrella policy reimbursed the firm for the missing inventory, and some embezzled funds.

Hanks could not recover the bookkeeping records, but there were paper files that helped him determine most of the data. Through the shipping companies, he could trace nearly all the shipments made from the warehouse over the previous few months. This gave him a handle on the approximate amounts of accounts receivable, and confirm the active clients.

The CEO candidate Martha was interviewing came on board, and he quickly reorganized the company. Within 60 days, the firm was functioning under normal activity levels. And over the next year it was back to the volume that Payne had reached.

Martha sold the company that year to a large competitor. The acquiring firm kept the CEO in his role and proposed a deal where she got a down payment of $750,000, and a monthly payout of $10,000 over the next 20 years.

She kept teaching until she retired as she loved working with children. Martha became close to her principal when his wife was diagnosed with metastatic breast cancer.

A year after her passing the relationship got closer, and Martha invited him to move in with her. They retired and took exotic vacations every year, but never married.

Salete Pereira

Six months after moving into her new home, Salete became restless. She had spent most of her time furnishing the luxury apartment and was looking for something productive to do. She had decided not to start up her decorating business again.

At church one Sunday morning, the pastor spoke about a program the bishop was launching to help orphaned children who were living on the streets. This struck a chord with her and after services, spoke to the pastor about volunteering.

With an offer of a large donation, she was invited to meet with the bishop. Salete suggested the diocese use the funds to purchase a building to house the homeless children. She was put in charge of the project and provided with a small team of volunteers. A priest, Father Lucas, who was liaison to the bishop was named her assistant. A building was quickly located, refurbished, staffed and furnished.

After managing the facility for a year, Salete had found her calling. She began replicating the shelter concept by buying buildings in other poor neighborhoods of the vast city. She was named executive director of the program and formed committees of successful business leaders and professionals. These teams managed fundraising, administration, staff management, education, and other services.

Salete directed this growing operation, which eventually housed thousands of young children, well into her seventies. At age 78, she succumbed to a massive stroke. The bishop, now a cardinal, personally presided over the High Mass at her funeral.

Barbara Newman

Barbara Newman left her employer the same year HydroDyne was sold. Her company's CEO often disagreed with her recommendations, insisting his own decisions be implemented instead of hers. In almost every case, his direction proved wrong and often expensive.

Frustrated, she confronted him, pointing out his shortcomings. But that only made the situation worse. She resigned and rebuilt her former law practice.

Over the next several years, Newman struggled to grow a practice that threw off enough profit for her to be comfortable. There were too few companies in the resort community that required her level of expertise in legal specialties.

She lived modestly until she reached retirement age. She bought a condo out of foreclosure in downtown Sarasota and enjoyed a quiet existence for her remaining years.

She occasionally reminisced about the HydroDyne chapter in her life. She had dodged a bullet when Dave Powers restored the company. He either never discovered her transgressions or chose to ignore them. Giving in to Gerard was one of the few regrets in her life. It made her wonder what might have been different had she stood up to him in the beginning.

Ronald Lawson

When Lawson could no longer take Gerard's abusive treatment, he abandoned his investment and never returned to the company. He managed the family trust funds and cared for his father. Two years later, he passed away, and the terms of the funds were modified. Most of the assets were divided among the siblings, with the remaining money set up in a few smaller funds.

Lawson was left with no active purpose, as he tried to adjust to an even more leisurely lifestyle. He bought a 42-

foot luxury cabin cruiser and after its maiden voyage around Sarasota Bay and into the Gulf along the barrier islands, it never left its berth at the Sarasota Yacht Club. He continued his visits to Costa Rica.

Lawson and his girlfriend broke up, and he never found a serious partner after that. He spent more and more time trolling the Sarasota bars and clubs, and eventually succumbed to alcohol, the same affliction as his ex-wife, that had caused his marriage to fail so many decades ago.

Diego Santos

After delivering his version of justice to Gerard Morbus, Diego still was not satisfied. The vengeance did not equal the pain Gerard had inflicted on his sister. To close the final chapter on this evil man, he wrote an untraceable email to the FBI.

The lengthy communication included the details of how Harold Payne had stolen millions of dollars and the entire inventory of Billings Battery Company in San Bernardino, CA. He explained that Payne changed his identity to Gerard Morbus and moved to São Paulo, Brazil, and later to Sarasota, FL.

Diego went on to tell how the greedy Gerard Morbus victimized the investors of HydroDyne Technologies in Sarasota out of millions of dollars. He described the mysterious fire that took Gerard's life and that of his girlfriend.

He ended with the name and account number of a bank in the Cayman Islands that held $400,000 in embezzled funds.

Three months later, Diego died in a shootout with DEA Border Patrol agents in Nogales, AZ. He was expediting a drug shipment from across the border and was caught in an ambush based on a tip from an informer.

###

Acknowledgements

In order to provide Executive Bone Yard its best chance for success, I recruited a team of talented people to assist me.

First was Salete Hinrichs, who inspired a key character in the book. As a native Brazilian, she taught me about the culture, locations, architecture and dining experiences in that vast country. I used her first name, her physical description and her personality as the model for the *Salete Pereira* character.

The patience and professionalism of my editor, Mark Mathes, was critical. His skill and encouragement made the novel more accurate, stronger and more moving in multiple ways.

My four beta readers were Fred Snyder, Barbara Somma, Mary Pat Piersons, and Alan Nimmy. Their insights added so much to the story development. And their early excitement and enthusiasm encouraged me to put in the extra effort to make this novel my best work yet.

Anne Young, Mary Forde and Gail Snyder and Larry Venable, all weighed in on the descriptive copy and the cover design.

Throughout the process, my wife, Sara played the role of my sounding board, reading versions of the manuscript, and noting areas of concern. She tempered my exuberance, and pushed me to add more descriptions and emotions to the story. And she used her typography skills to improve the text design.

About the Author

Michael A. Sisti is a serial entrepreneur, with 25 startups launched over a lifetime. All his books are based on his personal and business experiences, plus the constant observations of his surroundings.

Mike enjoys communicating with his readers, and suggests they contact him through his website. He also encourages and welcomes their reviews of his books on the site where purchased or reader sites like Goodreads.com.

Mike invites his readers visit his website and join his *Author Community.* By signing up, you will get a free eBook, plus newsletters, stories, perks, and other benefits.

As an accomplished speaker, Mike is a frequent guest lecturer at business conferences, educational events, service organizations and book clubs in person or via Zoom.

To reach him or learn more about any of the above, visit his website. And be sure to read his humorous and informative blog posts.

www.michaelsisti.com

Other Books Written by Michael A. Sisti

262

CPSIA information can be obtained
at www.ICGtesting.com
Printed in the USA
LVHW020357160421
684696LV00018B/959

9 780578 854892